PROJECT ARMA

LUCA
NYSSA KATHRYN

LUCA
Copyright © 2020 Nyssa Kathryn Sitarenos

All rights reserved.

Cover by Dar Albert at Wicked Smart Designs
Edited by Kelli Collins and Missy Borucki
Proofread by Jen Katemi

❀ Created with Vellum

Run. Hide. Don't look back.

Evie Scott went through hell and barely escaped. Now, she does everything she can to remain invisible. To survive. Because if she's found, she's dead.

Then she meets Luca...and there's a spark. But is he worth the risk?

Former Navy SEAL Luca Kirwin is both well-trained and deadly. Recruited into a non-sanctioned government project, he was unknowingly turned into a weapon. Now, he and his team have one mission—shut down the program.

When a new neighbor with haunted eyes moves in next door, his instincts tell Luca he can trust her. But could she be one of the enemies he's searching for?

As the couple falls deeper, and the danger gets closer, they'll have to learn to trust in each other...before it's too late.

ACKNOWLEDGMENTS

Kelli and Missy, thank you for putting the time and effort in to make this book the best it could be.

Jen, thank you for being the final eyes and catching any surviving mistakes.

Krista, thank you for always encouraging me to take risks, and reminding me that happiness should always come first.

Will, thank you for your constant love and support. You and Sophia are my everything.

CHAPTER 1

*E*VIE SCOTT GLANCED at her rearview mirror. Nothing. Not a single car, bike, or pedestrian appeared in her view. Did that mean there was no one following, or that they were good at staying hidden?

Nerves ate at her. Every time she stepped foot outside, even for a short grocery run, a small voice whispered that he was there, watching, waiting, ready to take her back. Keep her hostage again.

Detouring slightly from her route home, Evie played a juggling act between watching the mirror and the road. Eventually, enough calm settled inside her to pull into her driveway.

Taking a deep breath, she glanced at her small rental. Home. At least her home for now.

It was only last week that she had been sitting in a coffee shop two towns over, searching the internet for her next stop. It was there that she'd spotted the old house in the small town of Marble Falls.

The house was cheap. So cheap, most people wouldn't have spared it a second glance. For Evie, though, low cost meant affordable. Accessible. And that meant another couple months of anonymity. She could pay the upfront money in cash, and that was all she needed.

She would only be here for a couple of months anyway.

Comfort didn't play a role in Evie's existence. Survival was key. She would find a job, keep to herself, and move on. It was lonely. The alternative, Evie knew, was much worse. She would take lonely over that any day.

Pulling the door handle of her old Honda, she heard the hinges rattle, threatening to come apart. That was a worry for another day. She had bought the Honda at her first stop ten months ago. Even though the car was falling apart, it had still cost more than she had. She was grateful the salesman took pity on her and sold it for almost nothing. He must have sensed her desperation.

Or seen the bruises on her arms and face.

Stepping out of her car, Evie felt the sun beat down on her as she rounded the back of the car, opening the trunk to retrieve her groceries.

"Hey there, neighbor."

Gasping, she straightened, hitting her head on the trunk. The pain didn't register though. As she looked way up at the tall stranger, the color drained from her face.

Military. He was definitely military.

The man was tall, with muscles straining the fabric of his blue shirt. The real giveaway was the cut of his short blond hair. For some unexplainable reason, the cut always stayed with them.

A buzzing started in Evie's ears as she took a small step back. Her vision started to fuzz slightly, the stranger now appearing more of a blur than a man.

No. She couldn't pass out. The chance that he was working for *him* was too high. He would surely take her back. Even if she didn't pass out, how would she escape? He was huge. She didn't stand a chance.

The big man frowned and took half a step away from her.

That confused her. To take her, shouldn't he have moved closer?

"I live next door to you, in that house just over there."

Blinking a few times, Evie tried to ward off the haze and understand what he was saying. His body language didn't seem to be threatening, but that didn't mean he wasn't a threat. She hadn't thought Troy was a threat and look how that turned out.

Glancing around the yard, Evie half expected Troy to jump out from behind a tree. When there was no one, she turned back to the stranger.

The man in front of her shot a glance to the house next door. Glancing where he indicated, she struggled to comprehend the words he was speaking, the fear inside of her refusing to settle. Turning back to the large man, she forced herself to focus on his words.

"I just thought I'd pop over and introduce myself. See if you need a hand with the groceries."

With a frown, she looked back into the trunk of her car, taking a moment to consciously regulate her breathing. She'd spent months practicing her breathing and warding off the panic attacks. No way was she going to let one get the best of her now. Tuning into her training, she closed her eyes for a moment.

When she opened them, she felt the air entering her lungs at a slower rate and was able to reason. Looking up, she noticed the man was indicating to the house next door. He lived there. So, just a neighbor. A neighbor who clearly had a military background, but not a threat to her. Not right now.

Confusion swirled inside her. The man didn't seem fazed by her lack of response. Instead, he just stood there and seemed to be patiently waiting. Clearing her throat, she worked to find her voice. The embarrassment of standing there for so long replaced the fear.

"Um, thank you, but no. I, ah, don't need help right now."

Hearing the tremble in her voice, Evie struggled to hold the man's eye contact. Taking a breath, she waited for him to leave. When the shoes she was studying stayed where they were, Evie had to stop herself from nervously fiddling.

"My name's Luca, by the way."

Glancing back into the man's deep blue eyes, she had to stop herself from staring. They reminded her of the sky just before it rained. Beautiful.

"I'm Evie." Her voice sounded quiet to her ears. Would he have even heard her?

"Nice to meet you, Evie." The smile on Luca's lips sent warmth to her cheeks.

When he smiled, he wasn't so intimidating. He might even be able to fool people into thinking he wasn't a threat. Evie knew otherwise. His body spoke of power and strength. Most women, she was sure, would be all over Luca. Once upon a time, she probably would have been, too.

That was before.

"It's good to have a new neighbor here. The place has been empty for a little bit," Luca continued, glancing up at the house. "Are you from out of town?"

Forcing words from her throat, Evie nodded before she spoke. "I just moved here from a few towns over."

She had learned a while ago that being vague while sticking close to the truth was usually the safest course of action.

Her neighbor cracked another smile, and her heart stuttered. He was possibly the best-looking man she had ever laid eyes on.

"Well, if you need anything, feel free to stop by."

Without waiting for a response, Luca gave Evie one final glance before heading back to his place. The moment they broke eye contact, she felt like she could breathe again. As she watched Luca walk away, she noticed the muscles of his legs stretching his jeans. He was all power. There was also a lethal grace about him.

There had been another man in her life who had walked like that. He'd almost destroyed her.

At that thought, a shiver worked up her spine. Turning back to her groceries, Evie forced her mind to shut down any thoughts of her neighbor. He was military. Evie didn't need to be told that to know. She needed to stay away from him. Period.

"Never again," Evie whispered as she pulled the bags out of her car and headed inside. She would never again allow herself to be a victim.

Dumping her groceries on the kitchen counter, Evie turned to padlock the front door. It had been the first thing she'd installed the day she arrived. It gave her the illusion of safety. Illusion, because she knew no deadbolt in the world would stop Troy if he found her.

Time. That's why she'd installed it. She'd installed new locks at each house she rented. If he found her, she needed time to get away. What she would do with that time, she wasn't sure, but Evie prayed that if it came to that, she would figure it out.

Survive, that's all she had to do. That was the start and the end of her plan. It had been her only goal for the last ten months. Survive first, everything else second. And the first rule of survival was to keep moving. Troy couldn't find her if she didn't stay still.

This was Evie's fifth town in ten months. Five new houses, five new jobs, and five new towns filled with new people. It was hard, but not as hard as her life would be if he found her.

As she started putting away the groceries, her mind swung back to her neighbor. He had to be at least six foot three or four, a good foot taller than her. Not that another inch or two would make her any closer to his equal, physically.

Glancing down at her stringy limbs, she knew she'd probably lose a fight to a puppy. The diet of canned tuna and noodles she'd been rationing over the last few months hadn't helped. If Troy didn't get her, it was very possible malnourishment would.

Putting away the last of the groceries, Evie caught a glimpse of her resume on the kitchen counter. Lies. All lies. But she needed a job. A job meant money, and money meant survival.

Every move put a severe dent in her dwindling funds. Tomorrow she would find something. She always did. There was no other option.

About to move away from the kitchen, she paused, hearing scratching at the back door.

Her heart started to race. Evie took a knife from the cutlery drawer before moving forward. Glancing out the window, she saw nothing.

Strange. Maybe the months were finally catching up with her, and she was losing it.

Turning, she was about to step away when the scratching sounded again. Frowning, she looked through the window one more time, directing her vision down.

There, sitting on the mat, was a small golden mound.

Not hesitating, Evie unlocked the door. The instant it opened, the cat walked straight in like it owned the place and rubbed against her legs.

Quickly locking the door behind it, Evie bent down to stroke its back.

"Why hello there. Who do you belong to?" As her hand touched its mane, the cat arched its back and purred. Evie's heart expanded. She had always been an animal lover.

Not only was the cat thinner than it should be, it also wore no collar. Did it not have an owner?

Making a snap decision, Evie went to her cupboard and pulled out one of the cans of tuna she'd just put away.

"You look hungrier than me. You can have this can."

Emptying the contents onto a plate, Evie placed it on the floor. Confirming her earlier thoughts, the cat gobbled the food like it hadn't eaten for weeks.

"I'm going to call you Misty, and if you visit again, I'll share some more of this yummy tuna."

Yep, she was definitely losing it, talking about abducting cats.

Evie's eyes flickered to her laptop. Moving over to the couch, she opened it and found the encrypted file she was working on, resolve filling her. Cracking the file was her focus. It had to be.

Making herself comfortable, she felt movement on the couch and turned to see Misty curling into a ball beside her. Evie couldn't stop herself from giving the cat another rub. Maybe this town wouldn't be so bad.

As her fingers flew across the keyboard, she felt her confidence return. The answers were in there somewhere. The answers to why Troy had turned into the monster he now was. Evie would find them. No one could crack a file like her.

CHAPTER 2

NEVER AGAIN. WHAT the hell did that mean?

Luca Kirwin pumped his legs faster, trying to outrun the same sad green eyes that had been stuck in his head since yesterday. The two whispered words had been going back and forth inside his mind since he'd heard them.

He knew she hadn't intended for him to hear those words. She wouldn't even realize he was able to. His ability to hear what others couldn't was a blessing and a curse.

Shaking his head, Luca tried to push her face out of his mind. What was it about her that had him so captivated?

The look she'd had in her eyes alone should have sent him running. Fear. Fear of what, Luca wasn't sure. Was it just him, or was it all men that filled her with terror?

He knew he should drop it. Luca and his team had enough going on. But there was something inside of him that needed to discover the reason. Did she *know* him? Was she at the facility when he was? Had she worked there?

Shaking his head, Luca shut that thought down. No. He refused to believe that she had anything to do with that place.

Evie had the eyes of a victim, not someone who got their kicks out of gambling with people's lives.

Recalling the speed of her heartbeat, he wondered how often she felt that level of fear. He was definitely big at six foot four, and he kept his body in good shape, but he'd made sure to assume a nonthreatening stance.

An expert at reading people, Luca knew when to modify his behavior to encourage a reaction. Yesterday, he hadn't been able to put Evie at ease. Why?

"Yo, Rocket, slow down, man. Someone's going to notice how fast you're moving."

Asher's words cut through Luca's thoughts. Immediately he worked to slow his pace. Glancing around discreetly, Luca checked to see if anyone had noticed, relieved to see it was still just him and Asher.

"You're fine, brother," Asher said when he caught up, giving Luca's shoulder a friendly shove. "What's up with you today? It's like you forgot I was with you. And come on—no one forgets me, even on a bad day."

Luca glanced at his longtime friend and teammate. At a similar height and breadth, they might be mistaken for brothers. But where Luca was usually calm and controlled, Asher was more spontaneous. A risk-taker.

"I've got a new neighbor." Luca's voice was even. No one who heard him speak would think he had just run ten miles.

The shock was clear on Asher's face. That reaction didn't surprise Luca. The place was a dump. He had thought it would be vacant for good.

"In that old house that looks like it could fall over with a single push? Hell, I could probably give it a good shove and it would go." A laugh escaped his friend. "Hope they brought their toolbox."

Toolbox? He'd bet she'd packed one suitcase with the bare essentials. Ready to pick up and go at any moment.

"She shouldn't be living there. The place is a health hazard. It's not safe." Luca's voice was hard, leaving no room for debate.

"Perfect for those with little cash." Exactly what Luca was thinking. "What's got her stuck on your mind?"

When Asher gave him a side glance, Luca noted the smirk on his face.

Luca picked up his pace, Asher easily keeping up. "She's running from something. Or someone. I'm not sure."

Asher's expression went from joking to serious in an instant. It would have been the same reaction from any guy on their team. They were protectors first and foremost; it was why they had become SEALs. "You sure?"

With a slight nod, Luca kept moving, trying to wear his body out. Make it so tired his mind would stop thinking about her. But that seemed an impossible task since yesterday.

"I could tell by her body language. Looked like she was going to pass out at any moment. Just the sight of me made her want to run. Her eyes flickered around as if she was waiting for someone to grab her."

Asher flashed his gaze in Luca's direction before glancing back at the path ahead of him. Luca knew what was coming before the words left his friend's mouth.

"On the run? Scared at the sight of you? You thought about the fact she might be from the facility?"

"She's not."

Asher said nothing. The doubt in his eyes told Luca he wasn't in complete agreement.

"Meet her and you'll see." Luca kept his eyes ahead, subconsciously speeding up his pace again.

"We didn't even know we were being used as live experiments until it was too late. We trusted people we shouldn't have. Put our lives in their hands. Hard to trust your gut after that."

"I know." And Luca did. The whole team felt the pain of being used and lied to.

"It tears me up, man. We were SEALs. We should have been better than that. It took the fucking government exposing them for us to even know shit was going down." The rage in Asher's voice mirrored Luca's. "Then they think some hush money is going to fix it? Make us go away? Not gonna happen. I'm going to find every last person who had something to do with the project and make them pay."

"You're not alone, Striker." Luca used Asher's team name. "Don't worry, we'll find every last doctor, nurse, scientist, and soldier who thought we could be their guinea pigs."

Asher nodded, his expression steely. At that moment, he looked as deadly as they'd created him to be. A weapon. Just like Luca and the rest of the team. Project Arma had seen to that.

"We should start heading back. I'm taking the early class today." Asher's voice pulled Luca back to the present.

With a nod, they headed back to his house before they began work for the day.

The team used their blood money to open their own business, Marble Protection. It was where they taught self-defense classes and provided community security services. In addition to their own team mission of finding the missing members of Project Arma.

As they got closer to Luca's house, his mind again went back to Evie. Maybe he would catch another glimpse of her today.

"Is that your girl?"

As if conjured by his thoughts, Luca looked up to see Evie's face peeking between the curtains of her window. She probably thought they couldn't see her. A hint of a smile touched Luca's lips at that. He could see everything, from her golden-brown hair, right down to the spot of flour on her left cheekbone.

"That's Evie." The feel of her name on his lips felt right.

"I can see why you keep thinking about her." Asher's words pulled Luca's gaze to his friend. Realizing he wasn't the only one staring, anger rose in Luca's chest, but he wasn't sure why. He had no claim over her. Had only spoken to her once. Yet the thought of his friend admiring her made his blood boil.

"Eyes straight ahead, Striker."

A short chuckle escaped Asher, but he remained silent. Smart.

"I'm going to ask Jobs to do a background check on her." Luca hadn't even realized he was going to suggest such a thing, but now that the words were out, he knew it was the right decision.

Jobs, also known as Wyatt, was part of their team. He had a knack for technology. He was every bit as lethal as the others, but he had the added bonus of being a genius. If they ever needed information, he was their guy.

"Good idea. We can never be too safe."

Damn straight.

Luca knew the exact moment Evie realized he was looking at her. There was a slight widening of her eyes, and her lips formed an "O" as she gasped. The curtains were immediately drawn shut and Evie disappeared.

Holding back a chuckle, Luca slowed to a walk as they approached his front yard. Even though they had just run the equivalent of a mini-marathon, neither Luca nor Asher had broken a sweat. It had been a year since their enhanced abilities had taken effect, and the whole team was still discovering the full extent of what they could do.

"How's Jobs doing with the Project Arma file?" Luca asked. Their biggest lead right now was an encrypted file that had been sent to the gym by an anonymous source. Wyatt had been working on it for a while, to no avail.

"No progress yet."

Luca tried not to feel dejected by the response, but the longer it took, the further those they were hunting could run. They'd already been searching for a year, and all they had to show for their efforts was a file that seemed impossible to decipher.

"He'll get it, Rocket. When has Jobs had a file he couldn't crack?"

Luca needed to focus on that. Wyatt was a soldier first, closely followed by computer genius. He could hack anything...apart from seemingly this one file.

Entering the house, Luca and Asher headed to the kitchen for water.

With three bedrooms upstairs and an open living space downstairs, the house was too large for just Luca. The moment he'd seen that the property came with miles of empty woods as a backyard, however, he'd been sold.

As Luca opened the fridge, he listened for any sounds from Evie next door. He could faintly hear her moving around.

Since acquiring the ability to hear almost anything, the team had trained their ears to block out the sounds they didn't want to listen to, but for Luca, that didn't include Evie.

Both men moved to the kitchen bar.

"Want me to give Jobs a call about Evie?" Asher asked, opening his bottle.

"No, I'll ask him when I go in today."

Giving a nod, Asher was about to sit when a loud bang next door made them both stop in their tracks.

His body moving before his brain could catch up, Luca was stopped by a hand on his arm as he reached for his door.

"Knock, Rocket."

When Luca tried to pull his arm free, Asher firmed his grip.

"You don't know what happened, and you don't want her to see anything she doesn't already know."

Asher was right. Reluctantly nodding, he went outside and across the yard at a slower pace. When he reached Evie's door, Luca took a breath before knocking. "Evie?"

There was a sharp intake of breath on the other side of the door, followed by a shuffling sound. When that was followed by silence, Luca realized Evie probably wasn't planning to answer.

"It's Luca from next door." More silence. "I was just out the back of my place and heard a bang, wanted to check that you were okay." Clenching his fists, Luca had to forcibly stop himself from breaking down the door. The more time that passed, the more he thought of just going in.

Preparing to kick in the door, he stopped at the sound of her throat clearing.

"I'm okay." There was an awkward pause before she continued. "Thank you for, ah, checking."

Glancing back at his own house, Luca saw Asher's eyes narrow through the window. Ignoring his friend, he turned his attention back to the door.

"It would really make me feel better if I could see that you're okay, sweetheart. I could call someone for you if you'd prefer."

"No, don't call anyone!" This time her response was instant and tinged with fear. He heard her movement before the door cracked open, stopped by a chain.

Luca felt like he'd been sucker-punched at the sight of those green eyes. They had been stuck in his head since yesterday. The real thing was much better.

As he studied her, he was reminded of how small she was, at least a foot shorter than him. So damn fragile. There was no way this girl was the bad guy.

"I'm okay, Luca. Thank you for checking on me."

Their eyes remained locked for a moment longer before she shut the door.

Luca stood still and listened for any unusual sound. When there was nothing, he headed back to his house...and prayed whatever secret she was keeping didn't turn her into one of the people he was hunting.

CHAPTER 3

*E*VIE TRIED NOT to limp as she left the bakery. She had been walking around from business to business all morning, inquiring about job positions, but so far, no one was hiring. To make matters worse, she was doing it with an aching foot.

It was her own silly fault. She'd been trying to move a damn bookcase this morning so it was closer to the back door. She figured it would be easy enough to shuffle in front of the door, if necessary, to prevent an intruder.

Turned out the bookcase weighed a ton, and the whole damn thing had fallen on her. By "her", she meant her foot. Then, as if her luck wasn't bad enough, her good looking, dangerous neighbor had to show up at her front door.

That actually hadn't been so bad. No one had checked on her about anything for a long time. It was nice to think someone she'd just met might care what happened to her.

Evie had contemplated postponing the job hunt until she could walk without her foot feeling like it would fall off. But one glance at her near-empty purse had gotten her out of the house and knocking on the door of every business she passed.

Even though she could live on very little, Evie did require some level of income. She had always been able to find something in each town, whether that be waiting tables, making coffee, or even working as a receptionist.

Nervous tension filled her shoulders at the prospect of this being the first town where no one was hiring.

Doing some quick mental calculations on how long she could go without a job, her mind was suddenly pulled back to the present as she approached a building she'd already walked past a couple of times that morning.

At first it had appeared to be unoccupied, with its dark windows and lack of signage, so she'd disregarded it. But over the last hour, Evie had noticed quite a few people entering and leaving. Most had been wearing workout gear and clustered in groups.

A gym, maybe?

A sliver of hope rose at the prospect that it might be a job opportunity.

Pushing through the door, Evie walked up to the desk, hoping she didn't reek of the very real desperation she felt. Behind the desk stood a tall woman who looked similar in age to Evie. She had red curly hair pulled into a ponytail and was wearing activewear. She was stunning.

Evie tried not to feel self-conscious talking to someone who looked like they could be a runway model. As the woman glanced over at her, a huge smile spread across her face. Evie almost stumbled, surprised by the welcoming expression.

"Hi, welcome to Marble Protection. I'm Lexie. Are you here for the morning self-defense class?"

A wave of jealousy hit Evie. She would love to be as confident as this woman. She had been, once.

"Hi, I'm Evie." Trying not to be awkward, she pulled her resume out of her bag. "I was actually wondering if you're hiring?"

The girl cocked her head to the side. "You're new in town, aren't you? Well, of course you are, or I would have seen you."

Evie didn't know if an answer was required, but she decided it was safest to give one just in case. "I am."

Lexie gave Evie another once-over before her smile seemed to get even bigger, if that was possible. "Great! You might be in luck, Evie. I'll just call one of the guys down. Give me a sec." Turning her back, Lexie picked up a phone.

As Evie waited, a grunt from the left pulled her attention. She turned to take in the rest of the large space. The space was huge and covered in soft mats.

She turned just in time to see one man being flipped over the shoulder of another. Evie's eyes widened. The men were huge, both in height and muscle mass, and an audience watched them.

The man who was flipped jumped straight back onto his feet, seemingly unfazed by what had just happened, and crouched into a fighting stance.

Taking an involuntary step back, Evie felt a shot of fear at the sight of the violence.

Violence already filled her nightmares. It was what she saw when she closed her eyes or when her mind drifted for too long.

No. She couldn't be here. It would set off one of her attacks. She needed to get out.

Spinning around, Evie stepped forward—and hit a brick wall.
What the heck?

She flew backward before strong arms righted her. A brick wall with arms.

Glancing up, she realized that she hadn't run into a wall at all, but rather another huge man. Did this town have a factory of these men or something? Why was everyone so damn huge?

Then her brain caught up with her body. The huge man was touching her.

Pulling her arms free, she took a big step back. Touch from a man was another trigger for her. She struggled with any physical contact.

"Sorry, I thought you saw me behind you."

Evie tried to get her bearings as the man spoke. She looked up, realizing he was familiar. Had she seen him before?

The next moment, it hit her. The other runner. The man who had been with her neighbor this morning.

Now she *really* needed to get out.

Evie mumbled something that she hoped resembled a polite but dismissive apology and tried to step around him.

"Hey, you're Evie, right? You live next door to Luca?" The man casually stepped closer to the door, effectively blocking her exit. Not waiting for a response, the man continued, "Marble Falls is a small town. You can't walk five feet without running into someone you know around here."

Evie wanted to correct the man and tell him that she didn't know him *or* Luca. But that would encourage further conversation, and she wanted to leave. Now.

"Yes, that's me," she answered, giving a tentative smile. Her gaze flickered up to his face, then back toward the door again. She wished she was brave enough to slide past. The exit was so close.

"My name's Asher. Luca, our friends and I run this place." Asher gave what most women would describe as a million-dollar smile. To Evie, it just made her want to leave faster. Dangerous. That's what he was. In more ways than one. "What brings you here this morning?"

Crossing his arms over his chest, Asher looked like he was there to stay. He may as well be a statue. Resigned to the fact that she was now a part of this conversation, at least for the moment, she worked to maintain eye contact.

"Um, I just moved here. I'm walking around town to see if anyone's hiring. I didn't realize this was a fighting gym…or whatever it is. I was just leaving." Evie made a motion to move around him.

The polite response would be for Asher to thank her for stopping by, then step aside. He remained where he was, giving no indication that he planned to move anytime soon.

"Job hunting? Well, Evie, it's your lucky day, because we happen to be in search of a second receptionist."

Dragging her eyes from the door, Evie gave Asher her full attention. This place was hiring? What were the chances that the one place Evie *didn't* want to work was the one place that had a job available?

Chewing her bottom lip, Evie tried to hide the indecision she was sure was written all over her face.

"And we're a company that specializes in self-defense and security, not a fighting gym. Lexie probably mentioned we're called Marble Protection. We're your one-stop shop for all things security and defense." He flashed her another dazzling smile.

Evie turned her head and glanced to her right. The two men who had been throwing each other were now talking to their audience. The audience, she realized, was a group of teenagers.

Evie wanted to say no. Her mind screamed at her that being around these clearly lethal men wasn't a great idea. Being around violence was dangerous.

She spent a large part of her time on the run, trying to recover emotionally from what Troy had put her through, but the fear he'd instilled stayed with her every day. The very sight of violence in any form could trigger an attack, even on a good day.

But was saying no even an option? Her chances of getting another job in this town seemed slim. No job meant no money, and no money meant no rent, no new town, and not staying hidden.

If Evie didn't take this job, she would either need to wait around for someone to be hiring and hope she didn't run out of money in the meantime, or find another town with cheap rent that she could pay in cash. Not to mention the money she would lose from relocating again so soon.

Turning back to Asher, Evie knew the decision she had to make.

Instead of seeming impatient by the time she was taking, he looked like he could wait all day, just as Luca had yesterday. As she paid more attention, she also noticed he looked just as "former military" as Luca, as did the guys who were teaching self-defense.

"The job's yours if you want it, Evie."

Evie gave a resigned sigh. Survival. That's what she needed to keep reminding herself. She needed to survive until she could figure everything out, then hopefully, she could start living her life again.

If she'd survived the hell that her life had been a year ago, she could survive working in a gym with people who had scarily similar backgrounds to the man she was running from.

"When would I start?"

Asher's smile widened. "How about now?"

Evie tried to hide her surprise. "Ah, sure."

"Lex, wanna take your morning break and I'll show Evie the ropes?"

Lexie's head popped up from behind the bench, her gaze homing in on Evie. "Welcome to the team, new friend."

Lexie moved from behind the desk. Evie expected her to head down the hall. When she walked straight over to Evie instead and threw her arms around her shoulders, Evie stood frozen in shock for a moment. It had been a long time since anyone had hugged her. Too long.

Pulling back, Lexie held her shoulders. "Once I come back from my break, I'll show you everything that this guy missed."

From the corner of her eye, Evie noticed an eye roll from Asher before Lexie turned to leave.

"Women."

Evie didn't know if Asher intended for her to hear, but his words sent a touch of a smile to her lips. Maybe it wouldn't be all bad working here.

"We'll do all the paperwork at the end of your shift. For now, I'll show you the basics of how everything works."

Following Asher behind the desk, her gaze zeroed in on the high-tech computer.

"You hurt your foot?" Asher asked, not taking his eyes away from the screen.

Evie looked down, then back up in shock. She thought she'd been hiding the limp well.

"I just dropped something on it this morning," she explained, looking over Asher's shoulders at the expensive piece of technology. A bit of excitement filled her at the prospect of getting to work on that thing. Maybe there'd be more perks than just Lexie. "It won't affect my work."

"Didn't think it would, just wanted to make sure you were okay, darlin'." Asher gave Evie a wink before turning his attention back to the computer.

Heat worked its way up her neck to her cheeks. Asher was good-looking. Not as good-looking as Luca, not to her anyway, but he was impossible to ignore.

Focus on the job, Evie.

Turning back to the computer, Evie felt the tightening in her chest begin to release. After the eighth job rejection, the panic had been real. Finally, something was going her way.

Glancing again at Asher, Evie just hoped she wouldn't regret the decision to work here in the long run.

CHAPTER 4

"*D*IDN'T THINK IT would, just wanted to make sure you were okay, darlin'."

Luca heard Asher before he saw him.

Stepping into Marble Protection, *she* was the next person he saw. Evie.

What the fuck?

Stiffening at the sight of his friend and Evie in such an intimate position, Luca's hands clenched. Forcing calm into his body, Luca walked slowly but purposefully toward the gym desk.

"Morning, Striker." Luca gave Asher a nod as he approached. Narrowing his eyes slightly, he leaned against the desk. He turned his attention to Evie, his eyes softening. "Morning, Evie, didn't expect to see you here."

Evie's bright green gaze swung to meet Luca's and his body immediately hardened. He may not have expected to see her, but it definitely improved his morning.

"Well, you can start expecting to see her most days." Asher's voice pulled Luca's attention back to him. "Evie's accepted a job working the front desk. To take some of the pressure off Lex."

Leaning his hip against the counter, Asher gave Luca a smirk.

The asshole was still standing too damn close to Evie but Luca pushed that thought aside for the moment, focusing on what his friend had said. Evie would be working here. At Marble Protection.

Drawing his brows together, he stared questioningly at Evie. He was surprised. After his interactions with her, he wouldn't have pegged her for wanting to work anywhere near him.

It must be the money. She was clearly running from something, and that required cash.

"You're going to be our new receptionist?" Luca went for casual. With the stiffening of her shoulders, he may have missed the mark.

"If that's not okay—"

Before she could finish what she was saying, Luca cut in. "Evie." He offered an encouraging smile. "You'll be a fantastic addition to Marble Protection. Welcome." He held her gaze for a moment longer, not wanting to look away.

"I'm just walking Evie through the system—" Asher began as he turned back to the computer.

"I've got it." Not waiting for Asher to continue, Luca pushed off the desk and headed around the counter.

"You're welcome," Asher muttered. The asshole had a smile on his face as he spoke the words that he knew would only reach Luca's ears. Darting his gaze to Evie, Asher spoke in a louder voice. "I look forward to seeing more of you, Evie."

Then Asher disappeared around the corner, and it was just Luca and Evie.

Turning his full attention to his neighbor, Luca forced his body to relax. He needed to get a grip before he sent her screaming from the building.

"Ready to learn?" Moving closer to the computer, he brushed past her. Even that smallest touch sent a jolt of awareness through Luca.

With a small smile and nod, Evie turned her gaze to the

screen. Expecting her to put more distance between them, Luca
was pleasantly surprised when she didn't. Progress.

Knowing this was only the third time he'd seen Evie did
nothing to dampen his interest in the woman. There was something about her that pulled Luca in. He wanted to learn more
about her. And now he would have the opportunity.

Drawing his attention back to the job at hand, Luca started
explaining the company and their online system.

After just over an hour of taking Evie through everything,
Luca had a sneaking suspicion she had much more experience
with computers and technology than she was letting on. She
picked up on anything he showed her quickly.

At one point, when Luca clicked the wrong keys, Evie stepped
in and showed him how to correct his error in a way even he
wasn't familiar with. It raised more questions for Luca. Questions that he would find answers to. For now, he would be
patient. If there was something that being a SEAL had taught
him, it was patience.

Lexie had returned at some point, but Luca had directed her
to other jobs, not wanting his time with Evie to be disrupted.

Having gone through the proprietary online system, Luca
turned toward the open room. "Okay, time for the tour." Luca led
her away from the desk. His hand twitched with the need to
touch her. Guide her. He just restrained himself. Not wanting to
scare her.

Calm down, Kirwin. Get a grip.

Luca stepped into the sparring area that took up most of the
open floor plan.

"This is where we teach most of our group self-defense
classes. Asher, Bodie, and I tend to run the majority of the
sessions. We get a lot of school groups, as well as classes for the
public and one-on-one lessons."

Evie's gaze darted around the space. "How many guys do you
have running this place with you?"

24

"There are eight of us all together. We try to work to our strengths. Asher, Bodie, and I like to work with the community. Oliver and Kye do a lot of traveling for the company. They're away right now, in fact. Wyatt's our resident IT guru, and Mason does most of the administration and organization for the company. There's also Eden. He's more a 'behind the scenes' kind of guy."

Luca could see the questions behind her pretty green eyes. "When you spoke to Asher earlier, you called him something else."

"Ah, yes. We each have a nickname. Asher's is Striker, Eden is Hunter, Wyatt is Jobs. Mason goes by Eagle. Then we have Kye, who's Cage, and Oliver, who's Ax. Bodie goes by Red."

Nodding in response, Evie frowned, her brows pulling together. "What do the guys call you?"

Luca's lips split into a grin. "I'm Rocket, because I'm fast."

A hint of a smile showed on Evie's lips. "How fast?"

Leaning in close, Luca lowered his voice. "Don't race me; you'll lose."

When Evie turned her head, her lips were close enough that if Luca moved forward a fraction, they would be touching. That, he knew already, would send her running.

Straightening, he cleared his throat. "You can use whichever names you want."

"I think I'll stick to your real names, if that's okay."

"Of course, darlin'." He ushered Evie forward. As they headed down the hall, where half a dozen doors were located, he noticed she was walking with a limp.

Luca frowned. It was only slight, and the average person probably wouldn't have noticed it, but he wasn't your average person.

"Injure your foot since yesterday?" Luca kept his voice calm, but he was eager to find out what happened. The startled look on her face told him that she thought she'd been hiding it well.

"Asher noticed it too. You guys are very perceptive. It's nothing." Evie shrugged. When Luca didn't break eye contact, she squirmed before eventually expanding on the story. "I was just trying to move some stuff around, and one of the pieces of furniture dropped on my foot, but it's fine. That was the bang you heard this morning."

"Are you okay?" Concern coated Luca's words. The bang had been loud, and if it had been something landing on her, it must have hurt like hell.

"I'm okay, just a bruise." Evie eyed the hallway, clearly wanting them to move on.

"Anything else you need help moving?" Cocking his head to the side, Luca kept his face empty of expression. In his mind, though, he was hoping she would say yes. Give him another excuse to see her.

He felt the need to help this woman. Keep her close. He didn't know why.

Giving himself a mental shake, Luca broke eye contact. He needed to back off, stat.

"No, I've got it. It just slipped this morning. Nothing I can't handle."

Move on, Kirwin, the woman said no.

Letting it drop, Luca continued down the hall at a slower pace. "These rooms are used for small group and one-on-one sessions." He indicated the rooms on his left down the hall. "The room at the start of the hall, near the front desk, is the office."

Luca stopped in the middle of the hall, turning to the room on the left. He opened it to find Eden getting ready to work out.

Damn.

Before he could shut the door, Eden looked up. Of course he did; his hearing was as good as Luca's.

Silently scolding himself for not paying more attention, Luca wanted to turn around, but it was too late.

Eden gave Luca a quick glance before narrowing his gaze on

Evie. Fuck. Eden was not friendly to outsiders, particularly of the female kind.

The whole team had taken it hard when they'd found out what was really going on at Project Arma. Eden had taken it the hardest, however. Particularly because the nurse he'd been dating from the facility appeared to be involved, and she had conveniently vanished.

Standing, Eden took a step closer even as Evie retreated. Luca didn't blame her. At six and a half feet tall, Eden was the biggest on the team. The permanent scowl on his face for the last year did nothing to ease the intimidation factor, either. Right now, that scowl was aimed directly at Evie.

Luca's protective instincts kicked in and he placed his hand lightly on her back, even though he knew Eden wouldn't hurt her. Evie had a vulnerability about her. Something that made him want to protect her.

Without taking his eyes from Eden, Luca introduced them. "Evie, this is Eden, or as we call him, Hunter. Hunter, this is Evie. She'll be working at our front desk starting today."

Eden's piercing gaze homed in on Evie's face. Luca could feel the nervous tension radiating off her. He wouldn't be surprised if she turned and ran from the room right then and there.

Taking a subtle protective step in front of her, Luca narrowed his gaze at Eden. Evie didn't seem to notice, but Eden did. His eyes swung back to Luca, and his scowl grew even more pronounced.

Swinging his attention back to Evie, he continued to assess her. "How'd you hear about the job?"

For a moment, there was silence. The only sound in the room was Evie's thundering heart. Eventually, she spoke. "I didn't. I'm new in town and have been going to businesses today, inquiring about job vacancies." Evie gave a small shrug. "Just lucky I popped in here."

"I find luck doesn't usually have much to do with how things work out," Eden muttered. "So, you came in from the street, and we just gave you the job?" Eden's gaze was trained on Evie, but his words were aimed at Luca.

Stepping into his friend's space, Luca's tone chilled. "Calm down, Hunter. I've met her before. She's fine."

The two men stood face to face as a beat of silence passed. In the background, Luca heard Evie's breathing become jagged. Eden was scaring her. Luca probably was, too.

Turning immediately, he placed a smile on his face, strategically blocking Eden from her view. "Let's go, sweetheart, I've got more things to show you before you officially start at the desk."

Leading Evie away, Luca felt Eden's energy radiating around the room like a bomb about to go off. Making a mental note to keep an eye on Eden when Evie was around, Luca wasted no time shutting the door behind him.

CHAPTER 5

ONCE EVIE WAS on her own behind the desk, she fiddled with the computer, already feeling confident using their system.

"Look at you, all ready to go. Maybe I can finally take a vacation."

Jumping slightly at the sound of Lexie's voice, she turned to face the other woman, keeping a slight distance.

Lexie frowned at her reaction. "You okay?"

She hadn't been okay for a while. But that wasn't something her new coworker needed to know.

Forcing a smile, Evie nodded. "I didn't hear you walk behind the desk, sorry."

Giving a small laugh, Lexie turned to the paperwork in front of her. "If you think I move quietly, just wait. The guys may look like bodybuilders, but they move like ninjas. You'll never hear them coming."

"Thanks for the heads up." Evie hoped Lexie was exaggerating. She didn't want to jump out of her skin every time someone approached her.

"Where are you from, Evie?"

Shrugging, she tried to stick to the truth. "I move around a lot, but I grew up in Chicago."

"Ah, the land of deep-dish pizza." As Lexie reached for the stapler, her arm grazed Evie's body. She couldn't stop the flinch at the sudden movement. "Whoa, are you sure you're okay?" Lexie's worried gaze seemed to bore into Evie.

Darting her eyes around the room, she tried to think of a believable excuse. "Yeah, I'm just a bit jumpy. New job, new town."

Which wasn't exactly a lie. It just wasn't the whole truth.

As someone came out of the hallway, Evie looked up to see that it was Eden. Shrinking back slightly, she quickly averted her gaze.

When she glanced up again, it was to see Lexie studying her with sympathy in her eyes. "I'm assuming you've met Eden?"

Ah, yeah. Not the friendliest of greetings. Evie nodded.

"I've worked here since they opened the place. The guys are great, but I still don't know Eden very well." Leaning closer and lowering her voice, Lexie continued, and Evie had to make an effort not to move away. "From what I've picked up, he was burned pretty badly by his last girlfriend. He has mad mistrust of people now, particularly women. I don't know the details, but the guy's fine as long as you keep your distance."

"I don't think he likes me." Evie's voice was small, quiet, even though she knew it would be impossible for him to hear her.

"Join the club." Moving back to the papers, Lexie continued organizing. "Don't let it get to you. Every other guy here is great."

Stepping out of Marble Protection, Evie headed toward her car which was parked a block away. It had been a long day. First days always were. But the relief at finding short-term work was almost overwhelming. Plus, the job didn't actually seem too bad.

She'd been worried at the beginning, but the classes seemed pretty contained. The guys ran a tight ship at Marble Protection.

Lexie had been lovely, too. She was everything Evie wasn't. Confident, bubbly. Whenever the guys had come over to chat, she'd given them attitude but in a way that didn't take away from her charm.

Throughout the day, Evie had met a couple of the other guys who ran the place. Mason had stood out for his piercing blue eyes but quieter personality, while Bodie had been friendly and chatty.

Wyatt had been a bit more standoffish. Evie remembered Luca saying he was good with technology. How good exactly? It was a question that had been on her mind, but one that she wouldn't be voicing.

Evie had felt distrust emanating from most of the guys, even the friendliest.

Her mind flicked back to Eden, a shiver running up her spine. There was anger inside of him. Evie recognized it because Troy had carried that similar rage around with him. It had eaten away at Troy day by day. Was the same happening to Eden? Evie didn't know him well enough to tell.

In addition to learning the job, she'd made it her mission to avoid Eden. On the few occasions he'd come into the main area and been within sight, Evie had been quick to avert her gaze and appear busy. The feeling of having his eyes on her, though, was constant.

Evie increased her pace, a chill working its way through her limbs. The sun was almost finished setting, and it would be dark soon.

Evie hated the dark. She was automatically at a disadvantage with Troy at night. *Another* disadvantage, she should say. He could still see in the dark; she was blind. It was an extra layer of protection for him. As if he needed it.

As the echo of her steps filled the air, her mind flicked to

Luca. She could almost hear his deep voice in her mind. Over the day she'd started to feel more comfortable around him. It helped that he seemed to go out of his way to incite ease in her.

A smile touched her lips before she quickly shook her head.

No. She couldn't afford to trust him. She couldn't afford to trust *anyone.*

She should be grateful the rest of the guys didn't seem to trust her. It lowered the chance of her getting close to any of them.

Evie had just rounded a corner when the hairs on the back of Evie's neck stood up. A chill crept up her spine at the sudden feeling of being followed. Subtly, so as to not draw any attention, she turned her head to look behind her.

Nothing.

Taking a calming breath, she forced herself to maintain her pace, even though her legs wanted to run. She could see her car up ahead. Then she could lock the doors and have a semblance of safety.

Not far to go.

A rustling noise sounded behind Evie. This time, she did stop. Turning, she stared down the empty street. Again, there was nothing.

About to turn back, the sight of something flashing around the corner caught her attention. It was brief, but she'd definitely seen it.

Turning toward her car, this time, she did increase her pace.

Stop being stupid, Evie, it could have been anyone.

So why was fear coursing through her veins?

Jumping into the car, she immediately locked her doors. Air whooshed out of her lungs as she started the engine. It was hard not to speed as she drove home. All she wanted to do was press her foot to the accelerator and get out of there. She only just stopped herself.

Her rental was a good ten-minute drive. Every one of those minutes had her checking her rearview mirror a dozen times.

When she finally turned onto her street, she almost sighed in relief.

Parking in her driveway, she moved out of her car quickly. Just before reaching the front steps, she lifted her gaze to the house next door to see Luca standing by his open front door. His eyes followed her. Watching. His goofy smile from work was gone, replaced by a focused look of concentration.

Was it because she wore her fear like a mask on her face? Was the guy trying to work her out?

That lasted just a moment before his whole demeanor seemed to flick back to relaxed.

Evie had a sudden feeling Luca made an effort to appear less threatening and less dangerous for her benefit. Still, at the sight of him standing nearby, some of the fear started leaching out of her body.

She gave Luca a small smile before heading inside, immediately bolting her door. She leaned her back against it.

When would this end?

Closing her eyes against the threat of tears, Evie balled her fists. She was tired. Tired of the running, tired of hiding, and tired of the constant fear that threatened to consume her.

She didn't *just* want to survive. She wanted to live. Without the paralyzing fear of every shadow. She wanted to be able to walk to her car after a day at work without being scared of every noise behind her. She wanted to be able to see a man like Luca and have the courage to flirt, maybe ask him out like the old Evie would have.

Pain sliced through her chest, and Evie swallowed the sob that threatened to break out.

She pushed off the door, tamping down all feelings. She would *not* feel sorry for herself. She would not let Troy win. He'd already stolen enough from her. She would not allow him to take any more.

Evie made her way over to the kitchen, pulling out her

favorite mug. She would make herself hot cocoa and pray that it would chase away the chill.

She'd just mixed the cocoa in when she heard the same scratching at her door as yesterday. Checking the window, she saw it was the cat again. Evie opened the door, and this time didn't hesitate to lean down and pick her up.

"Hey, Misty, I'm glad you're here. I could use the company."

Feeling better already, Evie nuzzled her face into Misty's fur.

Heading back to the couch, Evie snuggled up with Misty and her hot cocoa and pulled out the laptop. She was so close to cracking the file, she could feel it. She wanted answers.

No. She needed them.

FASTER. *Evie had to move her body faster.*

Branches scratched her bare feet as she pumped her legs. Her feet pounded the uneven ground of the forest. Every so often her foot caught on a root and she stumbled, slowing her down.

The feeling of wetness soaked the soles of her feet. Whether that wetness was blood or rain, she wasn't sure. She hadn't had time for shoes. Only time to get out. To run.

Ever since he'd been back...since he'd changed...he'd never left the door unlocked. He knew she'd try to escape.

For months she'd been locked inside. A prisoner. Months of fear, of pain, of heartbreak. But today, he'd slipped. Whether he'd grown cocky that he'd catch her or complacent that she'd stay, she wasn't sure, but the moment she saw the unlocked door, Evie hadn't thought. She just ran.

She'd been dreaming about this day for months. She thought it wouldn't come, that she'd die in that house. She'd almost given up.

She had planned, though. Hopeful that the day would come. Evie knew exactly where she'd go and how she would get away, but she had to get as far as possible before he realized she was gone—because he was fast. Faster than he should have been. Faster than humanly possible. It was just another change since being involved in that project. Another mutation of the man she'd once loved.

The pain to her feet didn't register. She'd felt worse. He'd done worse.

The rain pounded down from the skies, softening the ground and making each step seem impossible. Her heart felt like it would beat out of her chest as fear almost choked her.

Evie didn't feel the broken rib that he'd given her the other night, or the fractured ankle from where he'd grabbed her two weeks ago. She felt nothing but the all-consuming need to get away. If he caught her, she would die. She felt it in her soul.

"EVALINE!"

At the sound of his voice, Evie's foot tangled with the earth and she tumbled. Not staying down long, she shoved her hands into the wet dirt and pushed herself up with an urgency she'd never felt before. Her feet stumbled a few more times on slick rocks and branches but she kept going.

Not allowing herself to look back, she focused her gaze ahead. She could just make out the highway between the clusters of trees.

That's what she had to get to. That was her goal.

The busy road where there would be people and safety. Safety for the first time in months...years even. There was no other option because if he found her, if Troy caught her, it would all be over.

Behind her, the sound of breaking branches and pounding feet made her heart lurch. He was here, and he was getting closer.

Another sob threatened to break out, but Evie pushed it down, forcing her exhausted body to run, to move.

The sound of cars gave her hope. She could almost see the vehicles ahead. Her body wanted to give out on her, begged for her to stop, to take a breath, but freedom came first.

Run now, breathe later.

That's when she saw the break in the trees, saw the flashes of cars and trucks. She was so close.

*"I SEE YOU, BITCH! STOP NOW, AND I MIGHT NOT BREAK
YOUR NECK."*

Pushing his words to the back of her mind, Evie focused on breathing. On moving her feet. She just had to make it to the road before he did. Surely he wouldn't drag her away with so many people as witnesses? Evie was betting her life on it.

"EVALINE!" He was close, so much closer than he should have been.

Just before Evie reached the road, she turned her head. She had to know where he was. Her breath hitched again as she made out his figure in the distance. He was almost a blur, he moved so fast.

Evie turned back. She had to focus. She couldn't let fear slow her down.

A couple more steps and she'd be there. Safety.

Evie pumped her legs for the last few yards and even as her feet hit the highway, her body wouldn't let her slow. She turned her head just in time to see the truck—

And the world went dark.

Evie's eyes flew open and she shot up on the couch, where she'd fallen asleep. That's when she saw him.

Troy. Standing in the hall.

Evie released a scream of utter terror that she wouldn't have been able to hold back if she tried.

CHAPTER 6

SOMETHING WOKE LUCA. What exactly, he wasn't sure.

Moving to the window, he stood for a moment and listened, trying to tune into the woman next door. He could hear Evie's heavy breathing. How he was so in tune with a woman he'd just met, he wasn't sure. But his greatest concern at the moment was the unnatural cadence of the breaths.

Then a scream pierced the night.

Luca shot across the room. Throwing on some shorts, he sprinted out the house and across his yard. He didn't worry about a weapon. He *was* a weapon.

Jumping the fence dividing his and Evie's homes, he raced up the steps. Stopping outside the door, Luca forced himself to calm. He called on his SEAL training and relaxed his body muscle by muscle before listening for any noise on the other side of the door.

The heavy breathing had returned, but other than that, silence. Only one breath that he could hear, which meant she was probably alone.

Even though it almost killed him, Luca knocked, not wanting to break in when things might be just fine. When he was greeted only by more breathing, he knocked again.

Speaking with a calm he didn't feel, Luca called out to her. "Evie, it's Luca. I heard you from next door. Are you okay?"

The breathing on the other side stopped for a moment before he heard her whisper his name.

"Luca?"

With a sigh of relief, he let his body relax at the sound of her voice. There was a quiver in it, but if she was talking, it meant she was there. Alive. He needed to see her, though. Now. "Yeah, sweetheart, it's me. You okay?"

There was a slight shuffling of feet before the door cracked open. This time no chain separated them. At the sight of her, he did a quick body scan from head to toe.

"I... I think, um, someone was in here."

He heard the terror in her voice. Saw the tight grasp she had on the door and the way her knuckles were white. Slowly placing a hand over hers, he untangled her grip from the door. "How about I check it out?"

Nibbling on her bottom lip, Evie gave a slow nod before she opened the door farther and stepped to the side. Good. She trusted him.

"Okay, sweetheart, you wait here."

As Luca was about to step around her, Evie's hand flew out and grasped his arm.

"No." Her voice was stronger than it had been moments ago. "I want to stay with you."

A wave of protectiveness filtered through him. Taking her hand in his, he stepped inside and placed Evie behind him.

"Stick behind me, okay?" At her nod, Luca moved forward. He'd never actually been inside, but he knew the place was falling apart. The paint was peeling from the walls, and there was a moldy stench in the air. It really did look as bad on the inside as it did on the out.

Was this even safe to live in?

Pushing that thought aside, Luca focused on the immediate first, then he'd deal with the house situation.

Keeping Evie behind him, Luca stepped into the living room. Nothing. Moving through the kitchen and toward the back door, he stopped.

There was a man's scent.

Keeping his expression neutral, Luca didn't let Evie know he suspected anything. As he moved past the window, he noted how easy it would be to open and close it without detection.

When he studied the lock on the door, his jaw clenched. A child could probably break through the thing.

Moving on down the hall, he quickly checked the two bedrooms and one bathroom. He found no other signs that someone had been there.

When he returned to the front room, Luca realized the scent of the intruder was…familiar.

Strange. He had no idea what to do with that information. He set it aside for the moment.

When they returned to the living area, he turned to Evie, keeping all emotion off his face. "All clear."

Dropping to the couch, she placed her head in her hands. When she looked up, her eyes were glistening with unshed tears. She looked so small and fragile that Luca had an overwhelming urge to shield her from whatever was causing so much fear and pain. He wanted to carry her away and rid her of the demons that were plaguing her life.

"I'm sorry, Luca. I had a nightmare, and when I woke up, I thought I saw Tr— Someone."

So, she'd had a nightmare, and now she was trying to convince herself that it was her imagination.

Standing, she rubbed her arms.

Whether she was trying to ward off the chill of the night or the terror, Luca wasn't sure. Likely both. And he couldn't stop himself. Walking over, he wrapped his arms around her, gently.

For a moment, Evie's body remained rigid, then she all but melted against him. She was soft to his hard, and so small in comparison. They stood like that for a moment, but all too soon, Evie started to pull away.

Luca reluctantly released her and stepped back. "Want to talk about it?"

Evie's eye's shuttered, and she shook her head. Secrets. She had many. She didn't need to tell him that for him to know.

"Thanks for coming over to check on me again. I think this is becoming a bit of a habit." A hint of a smile curved her lips.

"A good habit, I hope." Trying to think of a reason to stay for a while, Luca eyed the kitchen. "I could really use a cup of coffee if you have one."

Evie couldn't hide the surprised expression. Dropping her gaze to Luca's chest, she suddenly flushed a pretty rose color.

Remembering for the first time that he wasn't wearing a shirt, he knew he should probably feel self-conscious that his chest was bare. Having Evie's eyes on him felt too good, though.

Darting her eyes to the kitchen and back, Evie nodded. "Sure."

Luca followed her into the other room. In the corner, a solid bookcase was lying on its side, blocking half the space.

So, this is the source of her foot pain.

Righting the piece of furniture, Luca glanced up to find Evie's eyes on him.

"That was heavy. Like heavy-heavy, and you just lifted it like it was nothing."

Pausing for a beat, Luca casually shrugged his shoulders. "We run a tight ship at Marble Protection. No slacking on workouts allowed." His attempt at humor failed. Instead of the expected chuckle, Evie frowned, her brows pulling together.

"Next time, call me over. You shouldn't be trying to move something that heavy anyway. Now talk me through what happened tonight."

Evie's eyes turned haunted. Twisting around, she reached to fill the kettle. "It must have been nothing. My mind plays tricks on me sometimes. As I mentioned, I had a bad dream, and when I woke up, I thought I saw someone standing in the doorway."

"That doorway?" Luca nodded toward the hall that led to the bedrooms. When Evie nodded, Luca continued. "Do you remember what he looked like?"

Her eyes slid away quickly before meeting his again. Disappointment filtered through Luca. He had become an expert at reading body language and knew that the next words to leave her mouth weren't going to be the whole truth.

"Not really." With a quick shrug, she pulled the coffee out of the cupboard. "It was just a shadow. A man, maybe."

As Evie focused on her task, Luca noticed a slight tremor run through her shoulders.

"Is there anyone you can think of who might want to break into your home?"

Darting her eyes away from his again, she fiddled with the wood on the edge of the counter. "I don't… I'm not ready to talk about that, Luca."

Fair enough. At least she didn't lie to him again.

"You can trust me, darlin'. I know we just met, but that doesn't change the fact that I'm here to help if you need it." He wanted her to trust him. To confide in him.

When their gazes clashed, Luca could see the yearning in her eyes. She *wanted* to trust him. Probably wanted someone to help shoulder some of the massive weight she was obviously carrying.

She held out a coffee to Luca, her eyes shuttered again. "Trusting someone can be dangerous."

He took the coffee from her fingers. "Only if you trust the wrong person."

Pausing for a moment, Evie picked up her coffee, considering his words. "Is there a way of knowing who the right person is?"

No. But damn it, he *was* the right person, and he wanted her to feel that as much as he did.

As Evie placed the cup back on the counter, Luca reached over and wrapped his fingers around her wrist. "Go with your gut, sweetheart."

Her eyes glistened for a moment before she blinked away the unshed tears. Pulling away from Luca, Evie nodded but remained silent. She had that pensive look on her face again. "Guess that's something I'm working on."

Silence followed as they drank their coffees. His mind flicked back to the intruder that he was almost certain *wasn't* a figment of her imagination. Questions ran rampant. Who was he? What did he want? Is that who she was running from?

One look at Evie, though, and he knew he wouldn't be getting his answers tonight.

Luca took his empty cup to the sink before turning back to Evie. "Thank you for the coffee, sweetheart. You going to be okay?"

Her gaze shifted to his and softened. "Thank you, Luca. I'll be okay. The nightmare shook me a bit, but I'm fine."

"I can sleep on the couch for the night." Luca eyed the uncomfortable-looking piece of furniture, knowing sleep wouldn't be involved.

"No, no, that's okay. Really." Before he could push the issue, Evie opened the door. "Thank you so much for coming and checking on me. I'm sorry I woke you. I must have been loud. I hope I didn't disturb anyone else."

"I'm just next door if you need me."

He stepped close to her. Seemingly with a mind of its own, Luca's hand reached up and gently stroked her cheek. Soft. So damn soft. Leaning down, Luca placed a light kiss on the same cheek.

Was it just him, or had she leaned into him ever so slightly?

"See you at work tomorrow?" At Evie's nod, Luca turned to open the door before he did something stupid. "Lock up after me, okay?"

Waiting for her nod of confirmation, Luca finally pulled the door shut behind him. Once he heard the click of the deadbolt, he started down the steps.

Instead of heading straight home, he walked around the house, wanting to check everything out from the outside. Something made Luca stop. Crouching down, he noticed the broken branches. Ordinarily, they wouldn't have been cause for concern. But these led in almost a straight line from the forested area behind the house.

Quickly rising, Luca scanned the area, grateful his vision allowed him to see through the late-night darkness.

He was even more certain that there had been someone in Evie's home tonight. He looked back at the house and saw her figure moving behind the curtains she must have just closed. Lights switched off.

So, the asshole had entered through a back window.

Questions raced through Luca's head. Mainly, who was she running from, and why?

Pulling out his phone, Luca pressed dial. Even though it was the middle of the night, Wyatt picked up on the first ring.

"Yo, Rocket, what's up?"

Luca didn't bother with pleasantries. "I need a background check on Evie Scott, stat."

"Done. I'll have it to you by morning."

"Also, tomorrow, I want one of the team to sweep Evie's house for fingerprints and evidence. I also want new locks and a security system set up there."

This time, there was a pause before Wyatt spoke. "You got it." His friend still didn't ask any questions, and Luca was grateful for that.

"See you tomorrow." Without waiting for a response, he hung up and headed back to his place.

He wouldn't get any more sleep tonight. Not until he knew who his new neighbor was, and what or who she was running from.

CHAPTER 7

SIGHING, EVIE SIPPED her morning coffee.

Watching Luca's chest muscles ripple from across the room was fast becoming her favorite pastime. If she couldn't touch, she figured she may as well enjoy her view from behind the desk each day. It was quite a job perk.

Setting up the sparring area for the next class, Luca and Asher looked more like athletics models than business owners. Both were shirtless, both had rock-hard muscles, but only one held her gaze.

What drew her to him, exactly? It wasn't just the body of a gladiator or the deepest blue eyes she'd ever seen. There was something more. It pulled her in and made her want to break her "no-men" rule.

It had been a week since she'd started working at Marble Protection. A week of Marble Falls, bare chests, and Luca.

The day after she thought she'd seen Troy, she'd returned home to Luca insisting on installing a new security system in the house. She wanted to refuse based on expense, but he'd said that it would be a perk of working at Marble Protection. The knowledge that she would be a little safer stopped her from saying anything but thank you.

Picking up a pile of mail, Evie started sorting it. As jobs went, this one wasn't too bad. She hadn't met Oliver or Kye because they were still away, but all the guys, apart from Eden, were easy to get along with. They always said hi as they passed the desk in the morning and were happy to answer any of her million questions as she settled into the job.

Marble Protection ran like a well-oiled machine. The men shared most roles and helped each other when needed, as if they were family.

The thought reminded Evie of her *own* family—but she squashed it before the sorrow could take hold. Not today.

Glancing up again, she saw Luca had his back to her now, the muscles in his shoulders bunching.

"Checking out the muscle?"

Looking at Lexie, a smile lit Evie's face. A few of their shifts overlapped, and Evie was already starting to feel comfortable with the other woman. She hadn't had any girlfriends since high school. Talking to Lexie felt nice, taking away some of the loneliness.

"I wouldn't say that too loud; they might hear you."

Shrugging, Lexie leaned her hip against the counter. "So? Let them. They deserve to know that their twelve-packs are appreciated."

Taking another sip of coffee, Evie raised her brows. "Any twelve-pack in particular catching your fancy?"

Evie was referring to Asher, of course. She'd caught Lexie staring at him a few times, but so far, she hadn't specifically mentioned him. She actually seemed to go out of her way *not* to mention him.

Lexie narrowed her eyes. "Nope, I have an appreciation for every hot bod."

Giving a small chuckle, she saw Lexie's attention draw back to Asher again.

"He watches you too, you know," Evie said softly.

Rolling her eyes, Lexie pushed her hip off the counter. "Like Luca watches you? I don't think so." The sad tone in her voice was one Evie hadn't heard before. Lexie always made a point to be friendly and upbeat. "Anyway, I need to pop out to grab some more paper for the printer. Give me a call if you need anything."

Once it was just Evie again, she noted Asher watching Lexie's retreating form. Something was definitely going on between those two. She would bet her last dollar on it.

Darting her gaze to Luca, she found his blue eyes on her. A smile pulled across his face as Evie flushed.

Giving him a small smile in return, she quickly ducked her head.

Man, she was in trouble. She couldn't even look at the guy without blushing like a lovesick teenager.

She'd already spent a large chunk of her morning watching Luca from her living room window. It was a bad habit she'd started. Each morning, he'd leave his place at exactly six-fifteen for his run and return an hour later. He always returned looking like he could run another ten miles, not sweating, seemingly not winded.

And Luca without a shirt, on the move, was quite a sight. Just like the one here this morning.

Keeping her attention diverted, Evie focused again on the mail. Luca was too easy to like. Too easy to fall for—

"How we doing this morning, sweetheart?"

Evie spun, startled, knocking some of the mail to the floor. Had she been too preoccupied by her thoughts or had Lexie been right about these guys moving like ninjas?

"Hey!" Evie's brain scrambled to put a sentence together. "It's been pretty steady this morning... not too many calls. Everyone from your next class checked in."

Luca's smile widened. "Perfect, I love starting my day by scaring a group of youths into being good citizens."

Gosh, the man was beautiful.

With a wink, he turned to go, but not before bending down to pick up the mail she'd already forgotten about, placing it in her hand. The brush of his skin against hers caused a trail of goose bumps up her arm. The connection was electric.

Turning back to the desk, Evie concentrated on her work. As she finished organizing the mail, she noticed an envelope lying by her feet.

Lifting it, she was about to put it in the pile with the rest when something caught her eye. She could almost make out a logo on the paper inside. There was something familiar about it. Where had she seen it before?

Acting on instinct, Evie held the envelope up to the light to get a better look.

"What the hell are you doing?"

Startling, Evie spun around, the envelope falling from her fingers. "Eden... I didn't... I wasn't sure who the envelope was for."

He stood so close, Evie could feel the heat from his skin. She was dwarfed by his size. Trapped between his body and the desk, there was nowhere for her to go.

"If it's not addressed to you and no one told you to open it, then why the fuck are you trying to see what's inside?"

Squeezing her body closer to the desk, she felt the edge of the wood digging into her back. Her heart rate picked up, her breaths becoming shorter.

"I'm sorry." Voice small, she tried to stop the panic rising in her chest.

"HUNTER," Luca barked loudly from behind Eden, lifting some of the pressure on her chest.

As Luca pushed himself between them, Evie struggled to get

her breathing under control. The feel of Luca's warm back against her front went a long way toward calming her.

"What the fuck are you doing, man?"

No longer able to see Eden, she could still hear the anger in his voice as he spoke. "She was trying to read our damn mail."

Evie cringed as she tried to make herself as small as possible behind Luca. Expecting him to turn accusing eyes on her, she was surprised when he continued to face Eden.

"Her name is Evie—use it. And who the hell cares? What do you think she was going to do with it? I'm going to ask you again, brother. What the fuck are you doing right now?"

There was a moment of tense silence, and just as Evie thought her nerves would snap, waiting to see what might come next, she heard Eden turn and walk away.

Sagging against the counter, she let out a long breath. When Luca turned, she apologized. "I'm so sorry. I shouldn't have held it up against the light. It won't happen again."

Luca raised a hand to Evie's cheek, and she flinched away. A slight frown touched his brows, but he didn't voice his thoughts. Pausing for a moment, he continued to gently place his hand on her cheek. "Are you okay?"

Luca's soft voice and gentle touch soothed her frayed nerves. She hadn't expected...well, any of his reaction. His concern. His gentle touch.

Too surprised to speak, she simply nodded, not even sure her voice would work. Luca's thumb caressed her skin once before he removed his hand.

Immediately feeling the loss of his warmth, Evie wished she had the confidence to reach out and place his hand back on her cheek.

"Sorry about Eden. He's working through some stuff. That's no excuse for his behavior, but you're safe with me."

Still struggling to find words, she replied quietly, "Thank you."

Luca held Evie's gaze for another beat before slowly backing away.

Breathing out a sigh, she glanced down at her hands, noting how badly they were shaking. Her heart was still beating way too fast. She had come much too close to a panic attack. She had to calm down.

As she stood behind the desk, she practiced some slow-breathing techniques, trying to push Eden from her mind and focus on Luca's kind blue eyes.

She could still feel Eden's breath on her face. See the anger in his expression.

Troy used to do that too…tower over her, intimidate her. In the months before she fled, the towering would often be followed by a fist or some other form of abuse. Evie had learned to make herself as small and quiet as possible.

A shiver raced down her spine, and she turned her back on the gym and closed her eyes. "The past cannot touch me. It cannot hurt me. I am safe." She whispered the old mantra several times before she turned around.

After a moment, the violent trembling in her hands turned into a slight shake.

Good. That would fade soon enough.

Glancing toward the gym, Evie caught Luca's eyes on her from across the room. Their gazes locked. There was no way he could have heard that…but he had a primal look on his face. A look that made her feel stripped bare.

Evie was still holding his gaze when a shout came from the group of teenagers.

"Fuck off, Jasper, you weren't supposed to really punch me, asshole!" The kid—who looked more like a grown man—grabbed the guy opposite him, shoving him against the wall.

"Can't handle it?" The guy against the wall, who must be Jasper, threw out his chest, bumping the other kid.

In the blink of an eye, a punch was thrown, then the two were on the mats.

The punch came out of nowhere. Evie dropped to the floor, hitting it hard.

"You think you can fucking leave me, bitch?"

Blindly reaching up, she touched the warm blood trickling from her head, fear clouding her mind. As she tried to open her eyes, her vision blurred and bile worked its way up her throat. "You won't leave me. You won't even think about leaving! You're mine! You hear me?"

Before she could push herself up, a hand gripped her hair, ripping some from her scalp. The pain radiated through her head like a hammer.

"Get this into your head, whore—you are mine forever. If you ever try to leave me, I'll kill you."

The heat of his breath mixed with the warmth of blood which had trickled to the back of her neck. They were the last things Evie felt before he slammed her head against the floor.

"Evie?"

Glancing up, she could just make out Luca's concerned face. He was so close. She vaguely recognized that her breathing was labored. When she turned her head, everything else looked blurry. Like an out-of-focus camera.

Was Luca really here? But…Troy had just been here.

If he was here, she had to get out!

Closing her eyes again, she still felt Troy's breath on her neck and his hand gripping her hair. She scrunched her eyes tighter. Had to get him out of her head.

When a hand reached for her, she took a frantic step backward, hitting the desk.

"Don't touch me!" She heard the hysteria in her voice.

"It's okay, Evie. You're safe. Remember?"

Was she? She'd just heard Troy. Just *felt* him. She could still smell the blood from where he'd hit her. The shaking in her hands increased.

As the hand reached out for her again, she tried to fling herself back but was stopped by a hard surface. "Please," Evie begged. "Just leave me alone!"

She closed her eyes, saw Troy's hate-filled gaze staring back at her.

Oh God, she hated when he got that look in his eyes. Some nights she was sure he was going to kill her. Some nights, she *wanted* him to kill her.

Two strong hands suddenly gripped her arms. A scream escaped Evie's throat as terror took over. Covering her head with her hands, she begged for peace.

"Get away from me!" She couldn't go through it again. She wouldn't survive.

Confusion swirled through her mind. Troy's hands were... gentle. But Troy wasn't gentle anymore. Not since he'd returned.

"You're safe, honey."

The whispered words just reached her ears. They couldn't be real...but she wanted to trust them so badly. She craved for those words to be true. But how was she safe with Troy here?

Even if he *wasn't* here, he was alive, and that alone meant she wasn't safe. She hadn't been safe for a long time.

The air was no longer making it to her lungs, and she struggled to keep the panic from suffocating her. If she passed out, he would kill her.

"Breathe."

She tried to listen to the gentle voice. Oh God, she tried, but there wasn't enough air. Her lungs wouldn't cooperate. She gasped for breath, desperate to get oxygen into her body, but it wasn't enough.

Too quickly, white dots appeared behind her eyes. She was losing consciousness.

Evie prayed that if she woke up, the sweet voice assuring her she was safe would still be there. Too soon, the world went black.

CHAPTER 8

*L*UCA WANTED TO strangle someone.

Could no one in this place keep their emotions in check? First Eden blowing up about a damn letter, then those kids going at each other. It was like high school at Marble today.

Gently placing Evie on the office couch, Luca pushed her hair to the side. Keeping his back to the room, he heard the guys filtering in and knew that Lexie had just returned to cover the front desk.

Concern filled Luca. Evie's face was pale. Too pale. Tuning into her heart rate, he was relieved to hear that it had slowed back to an almost normal pace.

When the fight broke out in the gym, he'd heard a whimper from Evie. When he focused his attention on her, he'd first noticed her complexion, followed by her quick breaths.

It became obvious real quick that, physically, she may have been at Marble Protection, but mentally she was somewhere else entirely.

Luca had seen even the toughest of men have panic attacks, their eyes glazed over and reality no longer a factor.

There had been ghosts in Evie's eyes. There were moments where he'd thought she recognized him, but then she'd zone out again; retreat to some other place.

Coming back to the present, Luca turned to his Navy SEAL brothers. These men were his family, and he needed their support right now.

"Any idea what just happened?" Mason asked.

"She doesn't cope well with violence. She was already a bit shaken from Eden's little interrogation earlier." Clenching his fists, Luca felt his rage boiling at the memory of Eden standing over Evie. He was damn lucky Luca hadn't beaten his ass. He needed to back off before Luca lost his shit. She was not the enemy, and Eden needed to get that through his thick skull.

"She was holding the envelope up to the light, trying to read what was inside." Eden's apathy on the matter fueled Luca's anger.

"She's not our enemy, Hunter. Stop acting like she is."

Waves of violent energy flowed from Eden as he pushed off the wall. "She's hiding something, and you've brought her right to our door."

Luca moved toward him, placing his body between Eden and Evie. "How is she a threat to us? She's a five-foot-four woman who's done absolutely nothing to indicate she's our enemy."

Eden's body vibrated from anger. "Do we even know who she is?"

"I can't find anything on her." Wyatt ran a hand through his hair. "I think she's using a fake name."

Eden blew out a frustrated breath. "If she's connected to *them*, then her being here is a threat to all of us!"

There was a moment of silence in the room. Did the rest of the team think the same thing?

"She's not part of Project Arma." Luca said the words with absolute certainty. "You think I would bring someone in who's a threat to us? Who the hell do you think I am?"

Eden's eyes narrowed. "I think you're a guy who's making decisions with the wrong part of his anatomy, brother."

Luca struggled to keep his own rage in check. He had never hit one of his brothers out of anger, but at that moment, he was tempted.

"I know you've been through a lot, Hunter, but you better check what you're saying right the fuck now."

Before Eden could respond, Asher stepped between them.

"Let's cut the verbal sparring for the moment. Rocket trusts her, Hunter, so let's give him the benefit of the doubt until something proves otherwise."

For an instant, Luca thought Eden wasn't going to budge. The fury that radiated off him would've made an ordinary man quiver. Luca stood firm, unfazed by Eden's display of anger.

Finally, Eden turned away.

Regret filtered through Luca. Throughout all the training, missions, and life-and-death situations, they had never questioned each other's judgment before. Eden's recent past had really done a number on him.

Asher spoke up from the back of the room. "Still nothing more to report on her background check?"

Wyatt sank into the chair behind the large conference table. "Honestly, man, not a damn thing. Like I said last week, there's nothing to make us suspect anything. Graduated from high school eight years ago. Lived with her parents until the age of twenty-three, when she rented her own place. Worked in sales until moving here. Seems squeaky clean to me."

Moving back to Evie, Luca glanced down at her before turning to Wyatt. "Boyfriend? Partner?" There had to be something.

"Nothing in the system. She had some social media accounts but as of a couple of years ago, she was no longer active on them. Couldn't even find a parking fine, and trust me, man, if it was there, I would have found it."

That in itself was cause for alarm. What had happened to make her all but disappear?

And Wyatt was right. He had a brain that was technologically hardwired. You would be hard-pressed to come by someone better at digging up dirt than Wyatt.

Disappointment built inside Luca. Every day, he got a little closer to Evie, but not enough for her to trust him with the whole truth. He couldn't protect her if he didn't know what she was running from, damn it. What the hell was she hiding?

"What about her home intruder?" Luca asked, frustration eating at him.

"We've been back three times, Rocket," Bodie said, the same frustration in his voice. "Dusted every print we could find and found none but her own. Maybe they weren't after her?"

"The place had been empty for months, so ordinarily I would think it might be squatters thinking the place was empty. But what kind of squatters leave no prints?" Asher crossed his arms over his chest.

Asher was right. Something wasn't adding up.

Wyatt stood. "Her heart rate seems to be about normal again. She'll wake soon. Just keep an eye on her, brother. We're getting close to cracking the file. We can't afford a setback."

"Already done."

Wyatt glanced at Evie. "I hope you're right about her." He left the room, the rest of the men slowly following. Asher gave Luca a supportive pat on the back while Bodie gave him a nod on the way out.

When it was just him and Evie, Luca ran a hand through his hair and sighed. He wasn't making a mistake by trusting her. He could feel her goodness. She was hiding something, but it wasn't what Eden thought it was.

Luca sat on the edge of the couch. In sleep, she lost the constant worry lines that seemed to be a permanent fixture on her face. She looked peaceful.

Luca wished she had that peace more often.

Minutes later, Evie's eyes fluttered open. At the sight of her beautiful green gaze, Luca felt like he could breathe again. Looking around the room, it took her a moment to get her bearings.

Placing a hand on her shoulder, Luca scanned her face. "How are you doing, sweetheart?"

When she tried to sit up, Luca placed a hand on her arm to assist, easing her upright before she twisted slowly, putting her feet to the floor. "Did I...did I pass out?"

Gently moving a hand over her cheek, Luca nodded. "You did."

Evie's eyes widened. "I'm so sorry, Luca. I didn't mean to do that at work...in front of clients."

Keeping his voice low, Luca scanned her face. "Want to talk about what happened?"

Not hesitating, Evie shook her head.

Luca wanted to push. To question her until she told him everything. But he knew she would shut down first. He had to proceed gently.

"I'm going to give you a lift home." It was a statement. Not a question. Luca wasn't giving her an option.

"No, that's okay." She jumped to her feet before Luca could anticipate her actions. Stumbling, she absently reached for him.

Standing, Luca steadied her. "Whoa, darlin', you just passed out. Go slow."

Slightly panicked again, Evie shook her head. "You don't need to take me home. I'm okay. Plus, I brought my car."

"Okay, mind if I get a ride home?"

He'd brought his car but could get one of the guys to drive it home.

"Look, Luca, I'm okay...really." She took a step away from him, and he felt the loss of her touch immediately. "I'll be back at work tomorrow."

A chuckle escaped. "If you think I'm letting you drive home by yourself when you just passed out on me, then you must have me confused with some other asshole. There is no way in hell. I'm joining you—period." Luca gave Evie a patient smile and received a defeated look in return.

"Fine. You can drive my car." Her tone wasn't happy, but at least she'd accepted his help.

Luca stepped aside, allowing Evie to go first. As they headed for the car, the walk was made in relative silence.

Whenever he looked over to her, he could see she had that pensive expression on her face again. Her mind was elsewhere.

It wasn't until they were buckled into her car and Luca was driving that he decided to attempt a conversation.

"Tell me something about you, Evie."

Her gaze darted toward him, then away. Nibbling on her bottom lip, she seemed to be contemplating whether to tell him something or not. "I like computers."

Luca's brows shot up. It wasn't a surprise, he'd suspected as much, but he thought she'd share something trivial, like a favorite color.

"Makes sense. You learned how to use the online system at work pretty quickly." Evie's gaze dropped to her feet at the compliment, but Luca saw the hint of a smile on her lips. "What do you spend most of your time doing on computers?"

She shrugged, looking uncomfortable for a moment. "Not much. Just some gaming and stuff."

Lie. He could tell by the hitch in her voice. The slight elevation of her heart rate. Why would she lie about that?

"Ever thought about studying IT?" he pushed.

There was a long pause. Luca almost thought she wasn't going to respond when she finally continued. "No. I, uh…it hadn't really crossed my mind."

Another lie. Interesting.

The conversation remained light over the drive. When they reached Evie's rental, Luca parked the car in her driveway.

God, it felt like it had barely made the trip. The car was definitely on its last legs.

They were halfway to the door when Evie's foot caught on something, and she began to tumble. Catching her arm with his lightning reflexes, he held her close.

Her skin was warm to touch where her shirt had risen slightly. Luca could smell vanilla and strawberries. She was all soft and delicate, where he was hard and strong. He had to fight the urge to press his lips to hers.

"Go on a date with me."

It was a statement, but Luca still needed a yes.

Evie looked taken aback. Luca was a bit, too. He hadn't anticipated those words leaving his mouth, but now that they had, they felt right. Knowing what kind of response he'd receive before she even spoke, Luca patiently waited to rebut.

"I can't."

Wishing she would expand, he was disappointed when only silence followed. Not willing to give up so easily, he lowered his head and placed his lips next to her ear. "Go on a date with me."

He felt a shiver run up her spine. She turned her head, her mouth a mere few centimeters from his. Her warm breath touched his lips. If he just lowered his head a fraction, they would be touching.

The indecision was easy to read in her eyes, but beneath that, he could see the desire, almost a desperate yearning to say yes. She wanted him as much as he wanted her.

Deciding he didn't want to play fair, Luca pulled her even closer. "Say yes." He started a gentle stroke on the inside of her wrist as he whispered the words into her ear. "Please."

Be brave, sweetheart.

Trailing his mouth down her neck, he didn't touch her, but the promise was there.

"Yes."

For a moment, Luca thought he'd heard wrong. When the confirmation sank in, he wanted to run to the nearest cave and beat his chest. He decided to go with a more civil approach.

Lifting his head, he trailed a finger down her cheek. "Great, I'll pick you up in an hour."

Not giving her a chance to overthink it, like he knew she would, Luca took her hand and continued walking the remaining steps to her door.

"Today? Like lunch?"

"Yeah, sweetheart, today. Any foods you don't like? Anywhere I should avoid taking you?"

There was a short silence. "No."

"Perfect. I have just the place then." Scanning her outfit, his brows knitted together. "Wear something active; it's a bit of a walk."

Evie appeared surprised but didn't argue.

When they reached her door, Luca gently turned her to face him.

Every time he looked at her, he had to remind himself to breathe. She was so beautiful. Her wavy brown hair shone in the sunlight and her lips...so damn kissable. It was physically painful to be in her presence and not be touching her.

Tonight would be the first night of a deeper relationship. Evie just didn't know it yet.

Taking advantage of her stillness, Luca leaned down and placed a gentle kiss on her left cheek. Then he placed his lips next to her ear and said, "See you at one," before turning and heading across the yard to his house.

CHAPTER 9

HAT THE HELL had she been thinking?

Evie threw another top on the pile. Standing in front of the mirror, she placed her hands on her hips. Who gets told to wear activewear on a first date anyway?

Glancing around her room, Evie cringed. Almost every piece of clothing she owned lay either on the bed or floor.

Why was she stressing so much? It wasn't like she was going to date the guy long term. She'd experienced a moment of weakness and now had one date with Luca. That was it. Period. There was no way she would commit to another.

This could be good. Evie would go out with him, realize he's not the perfect dreamboat she believed, then she'd be over him.

Spotting a perfectly acceptable pale pink T-shirt on the floor, Evie yanked it up. Chucking it on over her leggings, she paired it with some white trainers. Turning from the mirror, Evie refused to give it any more thought.

There. Done. She should have done that twenty minutes ago.

Just as she started cleaning up the clothes strewn across her bedroom, a knock sounded on the door.

Was it time already? Looking over at her bedside clock, she noticed he was ten minutes early.

Well, there's the first mark against him. What kind of guy arrives for a date ten minutes early? Getting to a girl's house early on a first date was worse than getting there late.

Heading to the front door, Evie took a moment to calm herself before pulling it open.

Her breath hitched at the sight of him. He looked better than he did this afternoon. Wearing a tight gray tee that showed off his tree-trunk arm muscles and washboard abs, Luca paired it with running shorts and shoes.

Evie was in trouble.

"Sorry I'm early, didn't want to risk you running out on me." When Luca smiled, the dimples showed on the sides of his cheeks and his eyes crinkled.

Remember, Evie, this is a one-time thing.

She was not going to start a relationship with the guy. Men couldn't be trusted. No matter how good they looked in shirts that were two sizes too small.

Clearing her throat, Evie tried to settle her speeding heart. "That's okay, I'm ready. Should we head out?" Smiling, she stepped outside. As she moved closer to him, she got a whiff of his musky scent.

Oh, Lord have mercy on her, but he smelled good.

Stepping back, Luca placed a hand on the small of her back, and she felt the warmth seep through to her bones.

Evie slipped her keys into her pocket after locking her door.

She was kind of glad they were walking. He probably would have offered to drive had they taken a car, but there was the small chance he wouldn't have. Each time she drove her car, she had to say a short prayer that she would make it to her destination.

"Where are we headed?" Glancing down, she noticed for the first time that Luca was carrying a bag and what looked to be a picnic blanket.

He reached for her hand. A tingle went up her spine at the feel of his fingers wrapped around hers.

A voice in the back of Evie's mind urged her to pull away. Minimize contact with her dangerous neighbor...but she couldn't resist the small comfort.

That was fine. She'd show him she wasn't interested in other ways.

Realizing they were heading toward Luca's house, Evie frowned. Were they were having a picnic on his front lawn?

He turned and started walking around the side of his house.

Luca strode around the fence to the backyard, which led to the woods. Evie hadn't ventured out there, figuring she'd just get herself lost. Plus, it was a giant expanse. Anything could happen, and no one would find her for days.

Sparing a look at Luca, somehow, she knew she'd be safe with him.

"Come out here much?" Evie asked, guessing yes as she glanced down at his gigantic calves. He probably trekked the woods multiple times a day.

"Sure do. I love getting out in the fresh air. It's why I bought my place. I've got all this as my backyard. Feel like the luckiest son of a bitch around."

So the guy was sexy and loved nature. He probably had a secret stash of rescue kittens, too.

"What about you? Have you come out to explore since moving into town?"

"Oh yeah. I come out here all the time." Evie showed a hint of a smile.

Luca gave a chuckle. "You realize I know when you're not telling the truth because you crinkle your nose, then get this pained look of indecision on your face. Like you don't know whether to lie or be honest."

"Not true. I generally know when I'm not going to be honest. It's almost always premeditated." She laughed, glancing at Luca, expecting to see him laughing too. Instead, his gaze was serious. Intense.

"You can, you know. Tell me the truth."

Pausing for a moment, Evie turned her head away before speaking. "People only say that. They don't really want to know other people's baggage. If they did, they would realize why they were secrets in the first place."

"I never say anything I don't mean, Evie."

She let his admission roll around in her mind for a moment before deciding to test him on it. "Were you in a special forces team?"

There was no hesitation before Luca answered. "Yes."

She waited for him to expand, but he didn't. "Were the rest of the guys from Marble Protection on your team?"

"Yes. And we still are a team. You don't stop being a team just because you leave active duty."

Before she could lose her nerve, Evie asked her next question. "Were you a SEAL?"

"Yes."

Evie turned to see Luca's eyes on her. His gaze felt intimate. More questions rolled through her mind. Was he really the man he seemed to be? Was there a timeline on how long he would *be* that guy?

Exhaustion from being on the run wore her down. She was tired of carrying the weight of her past alone. There were so many nights when her secrets haunted her. Stole her sleep. Her sanity. To have someone there to offer comfort and an ear to listen would change everything.

What would he say if she told him part of her truth?

"My ex was a SEAL." She spoke the words quietly, as if they might fall on the wrong ears if said too loud. Looking again at Luca, she noticed his expression didn't change. Yet, at the same time, she could see his mind working.

"How long were you dating him?"

Too long. "Seven years. We started dating in my last year of high school."

Nodding, Luca's hand gripped hers a bit firmer. "That's a long time to be with someone."

"It is." A shiver ran down Evie's spine at the thought of the final years.

"What was his name? I might have met him."

Evie shook her head. As much as she wanted to bare her soul to another human, she couldn't. Not yet. "It didn't end well, and I don't like to think about him. Can we leave it at that?" She glanced at Luca. "Sorry, I shouldn't have brought him up. It's not really first-date material."

For a moment, Evie thought he wasn't going to drop it. Then he gave her a smile that made her knees weak.

"Did you know that you live a fifteen-minute walk from a magnificent waterfall?"

Evie's eyes widened. "Uh, no."

Luca stopped walking. That's when Evie realized she'd missed the sound of water. She looked ahead a short distance and spotted a river with a ten-foot-high rock cliff, water trickling down its surface. She couldn't stop the laugh that escaped her chest.

"You call this a waterfall?" Letting go of Luca's hand, Evie walked ahead, stopping at the water's edge. "I'd call it a stream with water dribbling off the rocks."

She turned and saw Luca setting up the picnic with a smile on his face. "Wow, you're hard to impress."

She lifted a shoulder. "I have high standards."

Turning back to the water, she closed her eyes and breathed in the smells of the forest. The area was peaceful. It almost quieted the voices in her head...It reminded her of summer trips with her parents, when they would go to the river. Their days would be filled with fishing and camping and roasting marshmallows by the fire.

"Tell me about them."

Startling, Evie found Luca right behind her. Damn, she must have said that out loud. Shrugging, she wrapped her arms around her waist. "What do you want to know? They were great parents. Always made me feel happy and safe."

"*Were* great parents?"

Turning away from the water, Evie watched the trees move with the wind. How was it that she had not only agreed on a date today, but was also sharing personal details of her life?

"They died. Home invasion. Two years ago." She met his gaze. When there was no pity there, Evie relaxed. She saw sadness in his blue eyes, maybe some empathy, but that was it.

"I'm sorry." Luca placed his hand on her cheek.

As if her body had a mind of its own, she automatically leaned into it. "Thank you." Her eyes dropped to his lips. Would it be so bad if she kissed this man? Everything in her felt the need to crush her lips to his.

As if reading her thoughts, Luca slowly dropped his head. She knew she should move away but didn't have the strength.

As his lips touched hers, all thoughts of retreating fled. The kiss was soft and gentle. She sank into him. Wanting more. Needing it.

Luca's strong arms snaked around her waist. Feeling his body against hers, Evie pressed her hands against Luca's chest, her heart racing at the feel of his muscles rippling beneath her fingers.

His tongue pushed into her mouth, and a soft groan escaped her throat.

Evie's brain told her to pull away, but the heat of his kiss was too consuming. His lips against hers were like nothing she'd ever felt before.

Other parts of her started to come to life. Pushing closer, she tried to meld herself with Luca.

Just as Evie's body started to overrule her brain, Luca abruptly pulled away.

She felt the loss immediately, opening her eyes in a daze. Luca's body had gone rigid, his hold on her waist tightening. His stare was fixed on the woods.

Realizing something wasn't right, her gaze darted around. "What is it?" She attempted to pull away from Luca, but his arms remained like bands of steel, preventing her from moving even an inch.

"I need you to wait here for a minute. Okay, sweetheart? Don't move."

Evie's concern increased at the hard sound of his voice. "Why? Is someone else here?"

Her heart rate increased.

Dropping his lips to her forehead, he placed a soft kiss there without taking his gaze from the tree. "I'll be right back. I'm just going to check on something."

Before Evie could respond, he was gone. He disappeared into the trees at an alarming speed. One moment he was right in front of her, the next, he was gone. It almost reminded her of—

No. She refused to go there.

He was a SEAL; of course he was fast. They only recruited the best.

Glancing around, Evie tried to calm her growing anxiety. Luca wouldn't have left her alone if he thought she wasn't safe.

Trying to keep herself busy, she finished unpacking the picnic basket, laying out dips, cheeses, crackers, and meat. Ordinarily, she would be drooling at the sight of all the food, particularly after her budget diet for the last year, but Luca's concerned expression filled her thoughts.

What had he seen? Was he okay? Where was he?

Once she'd finished arranging everything, Evie sat and waited. After what seemed like twenty minutes but was probably more like five, she heard rustling in the bushes and quickly stood.

Luca strolled out of the woods. His hair was windswept and his shoes muddy. Those were the only signs that he'd been running.

"Everything okay?" She heard the shakiness in her voice.

Automatically, Luca transformed from a man on a mission to someone without a worry in the world.

"Actually, no." Evie's heart rate picked up a notch. Then he smiled. "I want to taste you again, sweetheart, because you taste like honey and strawberries. That's a dangerous combination."

CHAPTER 10

"SO WE HAVE nothing?" Luca tried to swallow his frustration, but it had been two damn weeks. Two weeks and they still had *nothing*.

Wyatt cringed from his seat across the table. He and Luca, along with Eden and Bodie, were having a business meeting. Lexie was running the front desk while Mason and Asher ran a class.

"We followed the tracks as far as they led. We scoured every rock and crevice. We couldn't find anything. Whoever it is, beyond the tracks, he's damn good at keeping hidden."

"No shit. First he gets into Evie's house while she's asleep without even breaking a fucking lock. Then he manages to sneak up on us while we're in the woods. I heard his damn breathing; he was that close. Then I couldn't catch him. Who the hell is he?"

Bodie frowned from his spot next to Wyatt. "Honestly, man. I think that's a question for your girl."

Shaking his head, Luca looked away. "We've only been dating a couple of weeks. She's not ready, and I'm not going to push her. She's damn near ready to run as it is."

Pushing away from his spot by the door, Eden stepped

forward. "He outran you, Rocket. He got close without making a sound. He covered his tracks. He's like us. And if Evie knows what he is, then she knows what *we* are."

Luca stared into Eden's eyes, unflinching. "She's not ready."

Bodie shrugged. "If it was someone from the facility, they're doing us a favor, man. They're coming to us, instead of us having to find them."

That might be true...but they were also putting the woman he cared about at risk.

"Evie was there. If something had happened to her..." Luca stopped. Nothing would happen to her, he wouldn't allow it.

There was a moment of silence before Wyatt spoke. "You met her less than a month ago, Rocket. You don't think you're moving a bit fast here?"

Luca couldn't stop his laugh. "Trust me, with Evie, there is no moving fast. We've had a handful of dates and watched a couple of movies at her place. That's it. The girl's been burned. She moves slower than most...and that's fine by me."

Bodie gave a half-smile. "For someone who didn't meet the woman that long ago, you care a hell of a lot."

Trying to tamp down his annoyance, Luca grit his teeth. It wasn't their fault they didn't get it. "It's really not your concern. Evie's been through something traumatic, and it's holding her back. But I'm in this for the long haul."

"How do we not have any background information on her, Jobs? Her parents' deaths weren't even on the damn report you gave us." Eden's question was valid, as was the frustration in his voice.

Flicking his attention from Eden to Luca, Wyatt seemed to consider his next words. "I still haven't made any progress on her true identity."

"She's on the run and good at staying hidden," Luca said.

Wyatt crossed his arms over his chest. "Okay, but the fake

name comes with its own background that checks out. Someone who knows what they're doing put that together."

That stopped Luca in his tracks. Who had created the fake background? And more importantly, how had she paid for it?

Dropping his head into his hands, he ran his fingers through his hair. "I just need some more time. Please. I'll find out what we need to know, but I need to gain her trust. And whatever you're thinking about her links to Project Arma, they're not true."

"People aren't always who they say they are, Rocket."

Glancing up at Eden's words, Luca saw the hurt cross his friend's face. "I know."

"What about the Project Arma file, Jobs? Any progress?" Bodie questioned.

Relief filtered through Luca that they were moving on from Evie for the moment.

"I'm close, but not quite there yet. It's damn good encryption, I can tell you that." Picking up a short stack of papers, he tossed them to the middle of the table. "I *was* able to access some government files, some images they'd stored. These are pictures from Project Arma. We might be able to use facial recognition to identify and locate some people."

Luca was the first to lean over and pick them up. Rifling through the pile, he tensed at the sight of all the people he had trusted. Misplaced trust. When he reached the picture of their commander, he stopped, calling on all of his self-restraint not to crush the image in his hand.

"It tears me up that he betrayed us." Luca threw the image back onto the table. It sat there for a moment before Bodie lifted it.

"He was like a damn father figure. How did we miss it?" His voice held the same pain the rest of them felt.

"Like I said, people aren't always who they say they are." Eden turned toward the door. "Call me back if you find anything useful."

As he left, Luca released his breath. He felt for his friend. To have fallen in love with someone who was likely part of such a big cover-up would tear anyone apart. Eden hadn't been the same since.

"Any news on Shylah?" Luca kept his voice low, knowing that if Eden was listening in, he would hear.

"She's a ghost," Wyatt replied. "Since the government raided the facility, it's like she just disappeared."

"Do we really think she was part of it? She seemed like a pretty genuine person."

That was damn true, Luca thought, considering Bodie's words. Shylah didn't seem like your typical bad guy. But then, no one involved in the project had.

"By the end of it, we *all* knew she was hiding something about the facility. Then she just disappeared with the rest of them. It seems like too big of a coincidence," Wyatt continued, looking disappointed.

Silence filled the room as they each thought of how true that was.

Turning back to the pictures, Luca kept sifting through until he reached the last one. It was a group shot of his team in Peru, during a mission. Behind them stood members of the other SEAL team that had been involved in Project Arma.

"That was our last mission," Wyatt said from across the table.

Like Luca could forget. They'd returned to base to find people in suits waiting for them—and what they'd been told had changed everything.

"We never did find out why the other team had shown up on that mission," Wyatt said with a frown.

"I fucking hated those guys," Luca responded, tossing the picture on top of the rest.

Bodie scowled. "We all did. Not having to see their faces anymore was another bonus of the facility being shut down."

The two teams had never gotten along, largely due to the

other team's tactics. They didn't care if civilians got injured or killed during missions. They went in and got the job done, no matter the cost. That didn't work for Luca.

"The government thinks it's likely the team knew what was really going on at Project Arma."

"Not a surprise," Luca muttered, voice devoid of emotion. "They were always greedy assholes. Wouldn't have cared about the possible risks when they knew what they stood to gain."

"We need to find those fuckers," Mason said, entering the room and dropping into the seat next to Luca. "It's taking too damn long."

"You're right. We're doing everything we can," Bodie said.

"I know, man. It's just frustrating."

Standing, Luca placed a hand on Mason's shoulder. "We're all feeling it. We're going to find them. Every last one."

Turning, he headed into the main room. Passing the reception desk, he noticed Asher and Lexie were deep in conversation. When Luca walked past, they immediately separated. Then there was silence.

Strange.

"All okay over here?" he asked, glancing between them.

"Of course." Lexie flashed him a smile. "Guess who I'm visiting after work? Wait, don't guess, I'll tell you. It's one very pretty lady who happens to live next door to you."

Luca's brows rose in surprise. "You're visiting Evie?"

"Hey, don't sound so surprised. People can't help but like me." That was true. Lexie had a bubbly nature about her that made people relax. She could make friends with anyone. "I've been told I have a limited amount of girl time because she's expecting a certain boy after me."

"Yeah, so don't scare her out of town," Luca half-joked, turning his attention back to the gym floor.

"Sorry, can't promise anything, Luca. I have no filter, and if stories of you slip and scare her away, well...that can't be helped." With a wink, Lexie turned and walked over to the printer.

Glancing at Asher, Luca realized he hadn't said a word the whole time. He also hadn't taken his eyes off Lexie.

Realizing Luca was watching him, Asher scowled. "What?" Giving Luca a small shove, he headed back to the gym floor.

What the hell was going on around here these days?

"So, TONIGHT'S THE NIGHT, HUH?"

Evie took her eyes off the casserole dish for a moment to glance at Lexie, sitting at her kitchen table. "The night for what?" Playing dumb seemed the safest option.

"Don't pretend to be innocent with me, missy. You gonna bang the hot sailor boy or not?"

Almost dropping the spoon in her hand, Evie spun around. "Lexie!"

"What? We're friends now, and friends dish the goss."

Evie felt a pang of regret at Lexie's words. They *had* developed a good friendship in a short amount of time. The knowledge that Evie would have to leave sooner rather than later was a bitter pill to swallow. She hadn't had a friend in a long time, and it felt good to be able to relax and just hang out with another person, rather than her computer.

"Probably not. I can't get in too deep with him, Lexie." Trying to keep the regret out of her voice, she turned her attention back to the stove.

"Why the heck not?" Lexie seemed honestly confused. Evie didn't blame her. Most women would fight tooth and nail to rope in a man like Luca.

Taking a deep breath, she kept her attention on the food she was prepping. "You know how I told you I move around a lot? Well…I'll probably be leaving again soon."

There was a beat of silence before Lexie spoke. "I don't understand."

"I can't share everything, Lex. It's just better for me to stay on the move."

"That's bullshit, Evie."

Turning, she was shocked by the sudden sternness in Lexie's tone.

"You have a guy who really cares about you. You have me, who's a damn awesome friend. If you wanted to stay, we would help you with whatever it is you're running from."

Evie cringed. She hadn't told Lexie she was running from anyone, but clearly it was obvious. "I would stay if I could. You have no idea how much I want to." Desperate to change the subject, she noticed Lexie's phone light up for what must have been the tenth time in as many minutes. "Is that Asher?"

Frowning, Lexie put her phone aside, giving Evie a telling look. "He just... he annoys me."

Moving from the food to the table, Evie placed her hand over Lexie's. "I'm a great listener."

"It's just that every time I think we're breaking through the friends-with-benefits bullshit, he pulls away. It makes me feel like... I don't know. Like I'm not good enough for him." The insecurity in her friend's voice made Evie want to wrap her arms around her, then kick Asher's ass.

"If he's pulling away, then you're too good for *him*. Trust me. He would be lucky to have you."

Rolling her eyes, Lexie darted a look at the phone. "He's hiding something. Some secret that he won't tell me. The guys know. They're probably in on it." Shrugging, she tried to blink the tears away. "Just confirms my thoughts that he doesn't want anything more."

"If he's dumb enough to let you go, to not share his life with you, then it's his loss."

Lexie nodded before squeezing her hand. "Anyway, this isn't

about me." In a blink, the old Lexie returned. "Now tell me—are you going to do the guy or not?" When Evie hesitated for a moment too long, Lexie jumped to her feet. "I knew it! What the heck are we doing in the kitchen, girl, let's go find you something to wear!"

"I didn't say yes, Lexie. It's just dinner."

"Okay, whatever, let's go." Grabbing Evie's arm, Lexie all but dragged her to the bedroom. Once there, she went straight to the dresser.

Remaining by the door, Evie watched in stunned silence as Lexie, none too neatly, started rifling through her belongings.

"Girl, where are all your clothes?"

Slightly embarrassed, Evie shrugged. "I don't need much."

Pulling out what looked like everything in the top drawer, Lexie suddenly stilled. "Girl, we need to go shopping. You have nothing sexy."

Yeah, that's what happens when you barely escape a homicidal ex-partner.

"I guess these will have to do."

Lexie held up a black bra and panties. Her only matching set.

Evie's cheeks heated. "I'm not changing my—"

"Of course, you are!" Not waiting for confirmation, Lexie threw them on the bed, then opened the drawers below. "Now we need an outfit. Holy guacamole, girl, you're lucky you have me."

After a few more minutes, Lexie settled on a slinky black top to pair with tight jeans.

"This will be amazing. It says, 'I'm comfortable and not trying too hard, but just try to resist me.'"

Wringing her fingers, Evie looked over the outfit, then back at Lexie. "I'm nervous, Lex." So nervous. Like, drink-a-bottle-of-scotch nervous.

Gentling her expression, Lexie stilled before moving closer to Evie. "Of what? Luca? He's a great guy, Evie."

Glancing down at her hands, Evie said the next dumb thing that popped into her mind. "I've only been with one guy before and…he turned out to be not the best person."

That was the understatement of the century.

When there was nothing but silence, Evie glanced up to see Lexie's face full of compassion.

Taking Evie's hands in her own, she softened her voice. "Listen to me, Evie. The whole town loves Luca Kirwin, and since moving here, I can see why. He's a good man, and he would *not* hurt you. He's also infatuated with you. Just give him a chance."

Pausing for a moment, Lexie seemed to consider her next words. "I know you don't want to talk about it, but I think you were probably hurt badly by that guy. He didn't deserve you then, Evie, and he certainly doesn't deserve you now. But if you let him keep dictating your future, then he still *has* you. Have faith in what you feel."

On the verge of tears, Evie just nodded, not feeling up to voicing anything at that moment.

"Good." Flicking back to her usual upbeat self, Lexie grabbed the outfit off the bed and pushed it into Evie's hands. "Now, go put this on while I try to improve that God-awful-smelling thing you have on the stove."

With a small laugh, Evie headed into the bathroom, all the while trying to push her feelings of doubt aside.

CHAPTER 11

$\mathcal{L}$EXIE HAD LEFT after yet another text came through on her phone. Even though she wouldn't admit who it was from, Evie was almost certain it was Asher again.

With an hour to spare before Luca arrived, Evie switched on her laptop and got to work. She was closer than ever to cracking the encryption, but it was frustrating that she wasn't there already.

Her fingers flew across the keyboard, and she tuned the world out.

Coding had always come easy to her. It was where the world made sense. She felt confident when she was on the computer. The only confidence Troy had never been able to steal from her.

She knew that confidence was the very reason why he'd wanted her to drop out of college. That, and to isolate her. Make her depend on him. And she'd been young and stupid enough to do it. Wanting to please the boy who liked her.

Excitement filled Evie as she got closer and closer to her goal. When she finally opened the file, she would have her answers. What she would do with them, she wasn't sure, but she wouldn't spend the rest of her life wondering what had happened to the kind man she'd once dated, and why.

Maybe she wouldn't even blame herself for the death of her parents anymore...because there might be someone else to blame.

A short time later, there was a knock on the door. Realizing it was already time for their date, Evie quickly put away her laptop. One more week, maybe less, and she would have it.

On the way to the door, Evie felt a flutter of nerves. Glancing at herself in the mirror, she quickly pushed her hair behind her ear before opening the door.

At the sight of Luca, her mouth went dry. Either this man got hotter each time she saw him, or she was getting in too deep with her feelings.

"Hi." Her voice sounded nervous, even to her own ears. After knowing him for weeks, Evie would have thought she'd be used to being in his presence.

Luca's lips slowly spread into a smile. "Hi yourself, gorgeous."

Stepping into her space, he hooked an arm around Evie's waist and pulled her toward him. Before she had a chance to think, Luca pressed his lips to hers.

Dropping her hands to his chest, Evie let the outside world slip from her mind. This was her new safe place. Sinking into his kiss, she wished she could pause time and just remain where she was. His arms around her were like an anchor that stopped her from drifting away.

All too soon, Luca pulled back. A small groan escaped her lips. With a chuckle, he placed a kiss on her forehead. "You're killing me, honey." Moving inside, he shut the door. "Mmm, something smells good."

Heading back to the kitchen, Evie lifted the spoon, using a moment with the food to catch her breath. "I would love to take credit, but Lexie could see I was floundering and saved me. If she hadn't been here, there would be a very different dish served tonight."

The familiar arm once again hooked around Evie's waist from behind. "I would love whatever you cooked for me."

At the feel of his lips on the back of her neck, a shiver ran up Evie's spine. She leaned back as he worked his way down to her shoulder. Heat started to build in her core.

Squirming out of his arms, she put some distance between them. "Luca." She tried for a stern look but was almost certain she'd failed, based on the lopsided smile that stretched across Luca's face. "Stop. We're eating now."

"You're going to be the end of me, woman." With a last kiss on the temple, Luca grabbed plates from the cupboard. There was something about watching him move around her space that filled Evie with warmth. It was very...domestic. Something she tried not to crave anymore.

Troy had never helped with anything. In the early years, Evie was naive, wanting nothing more than to please him. By the end, she was almost desperate to keep him happy...because anything else meant pain.

A memory of the table not being set for dinner one night entered Evie's head before she could stop it. Her breath shortened as she recalled his hands digging into her arms and shoving her into the plate cabinet.

Quickly shutting her eyes, she focused on the smell of the food she was cooking, the feel of the spoon in her hand. *Stay in the moment, Evie.*

When a hand touched her arm, Evie cried out and spun around.

Sauce from the spoon went flying, and the utensil itself would have hit Luca in the head if he hadn't grabbed it from the air with lightning reflexes.

Luca's face filled with concern, and he quickly placed the

spoon on the counter. "You okay?" As his hand moved to touch her arm again, she flinched away out of habit.

Jesus. She was a mess.

Embarrassment filled her as she quickly turned to grab a washcloth. "I'm so sorry, Luca. I don't know what happened." Refusing to meet his eyes, Evie searched for sauce splatters as Luca watched silently.

After returning the cloth to the sink, she spooned some food onto plates and placed them on the table. She was grateful Luca hadn't said anything about what had happened, the time allowing her to regroup. But once they were at the table, the silence stretched out awkwardly. Evie racked her brain, trying to think of something to say that didn't involve crazy women who fling sauce around the room.

When her plate was almost empty, Evie finally worked up the courage to glance at Luca.

His gaze was fixed on her. Had he been watching her that whole time? She couldn't help but squirm under the intensity of his stare.

"Will you tell me about him?"

His words surprised Evie. Did he want to know about Troy? Could she tell him? She wanted to—oh God, did she want to. She'd never told another soul. She'd just run. Hid from it all. That had been her life for the last year.

"He hurt you, didn't he?"

She tried to hold back the tears that filled her eyes. Hearing someone else say the words made them somehow worse. She felt embarrassed without really understanding why.

Nodding, Evie whispered, "I was dumb for staying so long."

"Any man who hurts a woman is an asshole and doesn't deserve a single breath he takes." The fury in Luca's voice pulled her attention back to him. He looked every bit the deadly soldier she was sure he was at that moment. She could see the veins standing out in his arms as he clenched his fists. "As men, it's our job to protect the women we love."

Evie felt his words deep down.

Maybe that was it. Troy hadn't ever actually loved her.

Shrugging, she tried to downplay her feelings. Like Troy hadn't stolen everything from her. "I still could have left before…" Before he'd almost destroyed her. "I was stupid."

Standing, Luca moved around the table and knelt in front of Evie. He wiped away a tear that she hadn't realized had fallen. "If you gave your trust to this guy, and he didn't treat you right, that doesn't make you stupid, Evie. It makes him the dumbest son of a bitch on the planet."

Really? Because she sure felt stupid.

Looking into his eyes, she searched for anything to indicate he wasn't the guy he seemed to be. Everything she had experienced with Troy had taught her not to trust. That people can ruin you.

Luca's eyes spoke only of kindness.

Lightly placing a hand on his shoulder, she held his gaze. "You make me feel like I'm okay. And I haven't felt okay for a long time."

Running his hand up Evie's arm, he left a trail of goose bumps in his wake. "No matter what happens with us, you *will* be okay."

She felt the tears fall more freely. She'd tried to convince herself she would be okay, but had she ever truly believed it?

Wrapping his strong arms around her, Luca picked her up and stood in one motion, like she weighed nothing. Walking to the couch, he sat down with her on his lap.

Placing her head on his chest, Evie gave in to the silent tears. Now that they'd started, they wouldn't stop. Luca rubbed her back, and after a year of running, the feeling of safety wrapped around her like a warm blanket.

When the tears eventually stopped, Evie looked up at Luca.

He was so strong in so many ways. He made Evie feel like maybe she was stronger than she thought.

Could she really be okay? Could she trust Luca with her heart? The very idea filled Evie with both paralyzing fear and hope.

Reaching out, Luca wiped the remaining tears from her face.

"I must look terrible," Evie said, her gaze fixed on his soaked shirt. "I'm sorry."

Luca didn't hesitate. "You're beautiful." His hand cupped her cheek, and she pressed her face closer.

This man was unlike anyone Evie had ever met—and suddenly, she wanted him. Badly. She felt a need for Luca that she hadn't felt for anyone else. Wanted to know him as deeply and intimately as she could.

Making a decision, Evie straightened and lifted her mouth, placing her lips on his. The kiss was slow and gentle.

Moving her hands to Luca's rock-hard chest, she tried to deepen the kiss.

"Evie." She felt his hands tighten on her waist. "Maybe we shouldn't."

"I want to, Luca," she whispered, moving a hand into his hair. She prayed he didn't push her away, needing him both physically and emotionally. "Please."

A soft growl escaped Luca's chest as he slowly pushed Evie back onto the couch, engulfing her. She felt small under his powerful body.

Lowering his head, Luca sealed his mouth to hers.

This wasn't the gentle kiss she was used to. He took her; claimed her, the combination of his warmth and weight surrounding Evie.

As he deepened the kiss, his hand moved up her side, settling on her left breast. Arching against him, Evie closed her eyes. Finding her nipple with his fingers, Luca gave gentle tugs and swipes while his hips ground slowly against hers.

A moan escaped her lips and she flung back her head. Not missing a beat, Luca let his lips trail down her exposed neck, his warm hand traveling to the bottom of her top.

Taking his mouth off her for a moment, Luca pulled the piece of clothing over Evie's head. Throwing it aside, he continued his trail of kisses down her body.

At the feel of cool air puckering her flesh, she looked down to see her breasts were bare. Before she could question how that had even happened without her noticing, Luca dipped his head and took a nipple into his mouth. The sensation of his tongue against her naked breast made her toes curl.

Evie trailed her fingers down his back, her breaths coming out short. As Luca's mouth pulled and sucked on her nipple, his hand traveled south, unzipping the front of her jeans. Slipping his hand inside, Luca covered her core, over her panties.

The ability to think fled. When he applied pressure, it felt like too much.

"Luca." Evie hardly recognized her own voice, desperation all but bleeding from her. "Please!"

"Soon, sweetheart." His voice was hoarse, the need evident.

Slipping his hand beneath her panties, Luca rubbed her sensitive clit. A cry escaped and she ground her hips against his hand. She felt his hardness pressing into her thigh.

Reaching down, she tried to touch him but was stopped by his other hand. Taking hold of her arm, Luca pushed it against the couch, preventing her from doing anything but riding out the sensations flooding her.

A single finger slid inside Evie, causing her to jolt at the sudden pleasure. As the feeling intensified, Luca's thumb started a slow circular massage of her clit.

The aching inside Evie threatened to overwhelm her, the sensations all-consuming.

Luca switched his mouth to her other breast before sliding a second finger inside her and pushing deeper. Moving her hips,

Evie tried to ride his fingers harder, but Luca's body held her firm. The slow rhythm of his hand, coupled with the onslaught against her breast, was torture.

"Your little groans are killing me."

Evie couldn't respond. She couldn't think. His fingers moved faster inside her, deeper, and his mouth tugged harder on her breast.

She bowed her back and cried out as the explosion of her climax hit her.

CHAPTER 12

*H*OOKING HIS ARMS around Evie, Luca stood and walked into the bedroom, glancing down at her sated face. She looked relaxed and beautiful.

Mine. She's mine, and I'm hers, Luca thought. And he would make sure it stayed that way.

Placing Evie gently on the bed, Luca crawled on top of her. Her eyes slowly fluttered open. For the first time since Luca had met her, there was no worry etched in her beautiful green gaze.

"You're amazing," she said softly.

"If you think that was amazing, just wait and see what I do next."

A flicker of doubt flashed in her eyes before she quickly blinked it away.

Immediately lifting his weight, Luca leaned above her on his elbows. "Hey, you still with me, beautiful?"

Evie gave the slightest pause before she spoke. "I just... I don't have much experience." Looking embarrassed, she tried to roll away, but Luca's arms effectively caged her in. "And it's been a while."

"If you want to stop, you just say the word and we stop." Holding her gaze, Luca remained perfectly still above her.

"I don't…want to stop."

At the slight quiver in her voice, he started to roll away, then stilled at the feel of her hand clutching his arm.

"I don't want to stop." This time her voice was firm. "I want you, Luca. All of you."

Leaning up, she placed her lips on his. They were soft but sure.

Breaking the kiss, Luca covered her cheek with his hand. "Just so you know, you deserve the world…and I plan to give it to you." Lowering his head to her breast, Luca once again feasted on Evie.

Arching her back, she groaned. "You don't play fair, Luca." She gasped the words as her body writhed beneath him.

Luca felt himself harden again and urged his body to calm. He wanted to bask in Evie all night. Going up on his knees, he pulled off his shirt, catching Evie's eyes on him, desire and longing clouding her expression.

Fucking gorgeous.

Rolling onto his back and pulling Evie on top of him, Luca admired her breasts moving with the motion. Reaching up, he cupped them in his hands. Evie's head flew back and her little moans almost undid him.

"You are so fucking beautiful, Evie," he breathed, massaging her flesh as he spoke.

Heat built inside Luca as Evie's nails trailed down his chest. Wiggling herself down his body, she reached his waistband. With unsteady fingers, she undid the button before drawing down the zipper.

Luca didn't dare move, fixated on the glorious woman above him.

Lowering her head, Evie placed light kisses down his neck and chest as she reached into his jeans and clasped him. Luca's breath hissed at the feel of her touch. Evie's grip was tentative and exploratory. It gutted him.

Luca gritted his teeth and clenched his muscles in an effort to remain still.

As she slowly gained confidence, her movements became sure.

Raising her head, Evie claimed Luca's mouth. As her hand started moving faster, he held his breath against the rising surge of heat. Knowing he wouldn't last much longer if he let her continue, Luca flipped them over with ease, covering Evie's body with his own.

Quickly removing his remaining clothes, he crashed his mouth onto hers. He wanted to go slow, make this last, but he couldn't stop. He needed all of her.

"Tell me you want this," Luca whispered as his hips ground against hers.

"I want it, Luca."

Studying her green eyes, the mixture of lust and certainty he saw there was all the confirmation he needed. Without hesitation, he quickly rid Evie of every scrap of material left on her silky skin. Once she was completely bare, he took a condom from his jeans pocket and sheathed himself.

Slowing for a moment, Luca's eyes roamed her perfect ample hips, her small waist and generous breasts. "So damn perfect."

This woman was made to be his. Luca knew it with every fiber of his being.

He moved his hand between her thighs. With a gasp, Evie wrapped her legs around his hips.

"Please, Luca, don't make me wait."

Hell, neither could he.

With the patience of a saint, Luca positioned himself at her entrance and slowly pushed forward, not stopping until he was seated inside her completely. Then he remained still for a moment, not moving an inch. His body urged him to thrust, but he stayed where he was, enjoying the feel of his woman.

"You are the best surprise that's ever happened to me, sweetheart." Watching her expression soften, Luca slowly eased himself out, then slid back in.

Evie's breaths shortened, her hands tightening around his biceps. The feel of her hot core made him want to lose control, but he forced himself to go slow.

The pressure built as Luca continued his leisurely thrusts, his hand reaching for Evie's breast. His fingers found her nipple and he tugged and squeezed.

A cry released from her lips. Her hair splayed across the pillow as her nails bit into his shoulders.

Jesus, this woman undid him.

Luca increased his pace, dipping his head to her neck and feasting on her damp skin.

Evie's hips began to move, meeting him thrust by thrust. He flicked his thumb over her pebbled nipple, and Evie arched, her head flinging back. Luca moved his hand to her clit, his thumb rubbing where she was most sensitive.

More cries from her lips. More heart thumping against ribs.

Thrusting his hips faster, harder, he knew he only had moments left in him.

Suddenly, she began to tighten around him before a primal, almost tortured cry released from her throat. Thrusting deeper and harder as she came, Luca fisted the sheets and his world exploded.

Dropping down, careful to keeping the majority of his weight off Evie, he stilled, remaining inside her. The only sounds in the room were their heavy breaths and galloping hearts.

Eventually, Luca slowly slid himself out of her body, rolling to the side. Pulling her close, Luca shut his eyes and held the woman who had penetrated his heart.

About to drift to sleep, he was pulled back to the present as

Evie attempted to push away from him. Tightening his arm around her waist, Luca opened his eyes. "Where do you think you're going?"

Evie stilled. "I, um, thought I might have a shower."

Even though her eyes were downcast, he could just make out her expression. Was that regret? Pushing down the hurt, Luca sat up. "You mean you're getting the fuck out of here." He couldn't keep the anger from his voice, regretting it instantly when Evie flinched.

Shit. He needed to cool it.

Running a hand through his hair, Luca gentled his tone. "I'm sorry. Stay with me."

Evie bit her lip, indecision evident on her face. "I can't."

Luca knew what she was *really* saying. Not just that she couldn't stay the night in the same bed. She also couldn't be what he wanted her to be—his.

"Can't or won't?"

Turning her head away, Evie pulled the sheet up to cover herself.

"I want you, Evie, and I know you want me. You're scared, I get it. Someone hurt you in the past. But if you don't take a chance eventually, one day you'll wake up and realize how much you've really lost. You can't spend your life running forever."

Evie's expression shuttered. "You have no idea what my life is or what I'm running from."

Losing his patience, Luca raised his voice again. "So explain it to me. Goddammit, Evie, I want you to let me in! Let me help."

Watching Evie retreat into herself and shut down, Luca stopped.

He needed to go before he said something he'd regret. Standing, he searched for his clothes.

"Luca...I'm sorry."

Turning, Luca saw sadness in her eyes. The same sadness that was tearing at his chest.

"I want to let you in. I just... I need time."

Once dressed, Luca sat on the edge of the bed. Reaching to cup her face, a shot of pain ran through him at her small flinch. "I know, baby. I'll be here when you're ready. I just hope you will be, too." Placing a kiss on her forehead, Luca stood. "Lock the door after me, sweetheart."

Heading to the front door, he let himself out. He stood on the other side for several long seconds, waiting until he heard the click of the lock before walking the short distance home.

Was he falling for a woman who could never love him?

Luca blew out a long breath, not wanting to think about it. Because, for the first time in a long time, Luca felt real fear.

A LOUD BANGING on Evie's front door woke her. Squinting at the window, she noticed the sun was only just rising.

What was the time?

Reaching over, she grabbed her phone. It was early. Seven a.m. on a Saturday. Who would bang on her door at seven on a weekend?

When another bang sounded, Evie peeled herself out of bed and threw a robe around her shoulders.

Well, at least she knew it wasn't her ex. She doubted knocking on her front door would be his style.

She was halfway to the door when a voice sounded, causing a small smile to stretch across her lips.

"I know you're in there, Evie! Hurry up and open the door or I'm calling one of the guys to break it down. Hell, *I'll* break it down." Lexie's voice was loud, even by her own standards.

Sighing, Evie unlocked the door but only managed to get it halfway open before Lexie was pushing her way in. In her hands, she held coffees and a bag of something. Suddenly, her early morning intruder didn't look so bad.

Please let it be bagels.

Walking in like she owned the place, Lexie stopped at the kitchen table. "You really need to look into a new rental, Evie. This place is falling apart, and it's freezing in here."

Putting her hands on her waist, Evie rolled her eyes at her friend. "Lexie, what are you doing here at so early?"

"Well, good morning to you, too."

Sighing, Evie tilted her head to the side. "Lexie, it's great to see you and all, but I was sleeping, just like most normal people at this time."

Lexie placed the bag and coffees on the table. Evie had barely put the empty tuna can in the trash before she was reaching over and opening the bag.

God, it was blueberry bagels. She could kiss the woman in front of her. Maybe getting out of bed did have some perks.

Pulling one out, she started picking at it, knowing she would need her energy for the conversation she was likely to have with Lexie.

"I'm here early, Evie, because I start work in less than an hour and had to see you before I went in." When Evie didn't say anything, Lexie gave a huff. "Are you really going to make me ask? Did you bone the guy or not?"

Choking on her bagel, Evie gaped at her friend. "Lexie!"

"You did, didn't you?"

When Evie didn't respond, Lexie's shriek almost shattered her eardrums.

"Yes, yes, yes! This is so great! Tell me everything—and if you leave anything out, I will know and I will hound you." Taking a seat opposite Evie, Lexie grabbed one of the coffees and started sipping, her gaze unwavering.

With a shrug, Evie picked up the other coffee. "There's nothing to tell, Lex. He came over, we had sex, and he left."

"He...*left*?"

Evie so didn't want to talk about it. "Can we go over it another time? I really didn't get much sleep."

"What do you mean, he left? Like, he had sex with you, then just picked up his stuff and walked out?"

Squirming under Lexie's intense scrutiny, Evie almost couldn't meet her friend's gaze. "Not exactly. We had sex, then I went to get up. Luca didn't like it and he...left."

Lexie's eyes narrowed. "You went to get up and go *where?*"

"I don't know. To have a shower?"

Lexie's mind seemed to be working overtime, clicking everything into place. "How soon after did you get up?"

Oh, heck. "Straight after."

Shooting to her feet, Lexie almost caused Evie to drop her coffee.

"What the heck, Evie? You *like* the guy. I know you do. You finally get close to him, and then you push him away again?"

"I didn't push him away."

"Like hell you didn't." The anger in Lexie's voice surprised Evie. "This perfect man wants to spend the night with you, and you treat him like you just want him for...what? Sex?"

"That isn't true." Placing her coffee and bagel on the table, Evie crossed her arms. "He knows that I don't want to be in a relationship. He shouldn't have been surprised."

Shaking her head, Lexie glanced toward the ceiling. "Lord, give me patience."

A scratching sounded at the back door, followed by a loud purring.

Spinning, Lexie's eyes got big. "What the heck is that?"

Rising to her feet, Evie moved to the door. "It's Misty."

"Misty?"

"The cat that comes over. I don't think she has an owner, so I've just sort of adopted her." She opened the door and Misty walked in. Evie didn't hesitate to pick her up. Scratching her head, Evie buried her face in the soft fur.

A gasp from Lexie pulled her attention.

"Oh God, you're going to turn into a lonely cat lady." Before Evie could rebut, Lexie shook her head as she picked up her coffee and keys. "Nope, I'm not gonna let it happen. We're going out tonight."

Evie's eyes widened. "Where are we going?"

The sparkle in Lexie's eyes did nothing to reassure her. "Never you mind. I'll be back around eight tonight to pick you up. Don't worry about picking an outfit, I'll bring you something."

Feeling the familiar panic, Evie tried to reason with her friend. "Lex, I can't."

Lexie walked over to Evie, her voice gentling. "It will be fun. Something I think you need more of in your life."

Would it? Lexie was right, there hadn't been a lot of fun in Evie's life. Hell, there hadn't been *any* in the last few years. "Okay."

The moment the word was out, a large smile stretched across her friend's lips. "Great! I'm so excited." She gave Evie a big hug before heading to the door. "I'm off to watch some sexy men at work for the day. Eat the second bagel, you'll need your energy."

Then she was gone, leaving Evie wondering what had just happened.

CHAPTER 13

*E*VIE TRIED NOT to feel out of place as Lexie pulled her into the bar. Her experience with going to bars was limited, and Lexie was throwing her into the deep end. The place was packed. Almost all the booths along the wall, as well as the scattered tables, were taken. The dance floor was also filled with people.

So, this is what people do on a Saturday night in Marble Falls.

Walking up to the bar, Evie tugged at the bottom of her skirt. No, not her skirt, Lexie's. True to her word, her friend had shown up with a skirt, top, and matching heels, obviously knowing Evie's ability to look sexy on her own was pretty much non-existent.

Catching Evie in the act, Lexie turned from the bar to face her friend. "Stop. You look hot. Just relax and have fun tonight. Okay?"

Before she was able to respond, the bartender interrupted.

"What can I get for you ladies?" A tall man with tattoos down his arms stood in front of them. He was attractive, in a rough biker kind of way. Definitely not Evie's type.

"Why hello there. My girlfriend and I would like whatever

drink will get us drunk fastest." Lexie glanced at Evie, daring her to argue. "Accept it, this is happening."

Not looking fazed at all, the bartender nodded. "You got it." Picking up bottles, he started pouring.

Well, it didn't look like this was the first time he'd had that request. "Isn't he going to tell us what he's making?"

"We know what he's making, Evie. Something to make this night one to remember...or maybe *not* remember."

Lexie chuckled as two glasses of blue liquid were set in front of them. Apprehension crept into Evie, especially when he grabbed two shot glasses and poured what looked like whiskey. Giving Lexie a once-over, he pushed the two shots next to the drinks.

"Shots are on the house."

Lexie smiled before paying for their drinks. Picking up both shot glasses, she turned to Evie and placed one in her hand. Lifting her own shot, Lexie raised her voice. "Tonight, we say fuck men, and we have a good time." After clinking her glass against Evie's, Lexie tossed back the shot.

Taking a more cautious approach, Evie gave the glass a sniff first. Yep, definitely whiskey.

Scrunching her eyes shut, Evie downed the shot. The hard liquor burned her throat, and she had to force herself not to gag. "That was disgusting, Lex."

Lexie showed no sympathy. If anything, she seemed pleased with her assessment. "Haven't you heard the saying, Evie? The more horrid the taste, the better the drink."

Evie was sure that was *not* a saying. But she was equally sure that arguing would get her nowhere.

Lifting the mysterious blue drink, Evie cradled the glass. She would wait a couple of minutes before taking the plunge. Already feeling the whiskey warming her insides, she knew she'd have to be careful. A lightweight when it came to drinking in high school, she was sure that hadn't improved by her years of abstinence.

Realizing what Lexie had said, she studied her friend. "Why are *you* saying fuck men?"

Rolling her eyes, Lexie took a big gulp of her drink. "I'm over Asher and his lies. Last night, I straight-out asked him what the big secret was, and do you know what he told me? That he just wasn't a commitment guy."

Lexie took another big gulp of her drink. Maybe it wasn't herself Evie should be worried about.

"First of all, I never said I wanted to marry the guy, just have a semi-functional relationship. Second, I can tell he's keeping something from me, so he either needs to tell me or get lost! Anyway, let's get drunk and dance. Maybe I'll meet a nice guy here who wants to commit to me."

Hooking her arm through Evie's before she had a chance to respond, Lexie led them into the dense crowd.

"Some people have good reasons for keeping secrets, Lex. Maybe you should just give it some time and he'll come around."

"Yeah, and maybe pigs will fly," Lexie muttered, more to herself than anyone else.

Partway to the dance floor, they were stopped by two mammoth people who stepped in front of them. Make that *familiar* mammoth people.

Evie looked way up at Mason and Eden. They both stood a good head taller than just about everyone else in the room.

Reconsidering her earlier thoughts on going slow, Evie gulped down half of whatever was in her drink, deciding the liquid confidence was definitely needed.

Not seeming perturbed, Lexie spoke first. "Hey, boys, what are you doing here?"

Taking a drink of his beer, Mason gave a shrug. "Not much, actually. I didn't know you guys hung out."

Lexie kept the friendliness in her voice, but it had a bit of edge this time. "Why wouldn't we?"

Taking another sip of her drink, Evie started to feel a bit more relaxed. Good, the alcohol was taking effect. Looking down, she vaguely wondered how *much* alcohol it contained, exactly.

"You're different, is all," Mason said with a shrug. Evie had forgotten what the question was.

"We're not that different, are we, Evie?" Lexie put her arm around Evie's shoulders, pulling her close.

Evie braved a glance at Eden. Yep, staring directly at her. Sipping her drink, she shook her head.

"See?" Lexie responded, not seeming bothered that she had to do most of the talking.

Mason gave a chuckle. "Women. I'll never understand you guys." Taking another swig of his beer, he continued. "Do Asher and Luca know you're both here tonight?"

Lexie's body stiffened.

Ah, no. Wrong question, buddy.

Knowing what was coming, Evie tried to tune the conversation out as Lexie raised her voice at Mason.

Glancing around the bar, she again noticed how truly packed it was. Was it always this busy on a Saturday? She wouldn't have thought so many people could even fit in such a small room. As she turned her attention back to Mason, something caught her eye.

Quickly glancing around, she tried to figure out what it was she'd seen.

Then she spotted it again. A flash of a jacket before the man turned. It looked just like one she'd bought for Troy years ago. It was custom made. She'd gotten "T.T." for Troy Turner embroidered on the right shoulder their first Christmas together.

Evie's entire body chilled. It couldn't be. How was the jacket here now? In this room?

She didn't know if it was the alcohol that fueled her confidence, but she suddenly needed to know if it was him.

Turning away from her group, Evie started pushing her way through the crowd. She could just make out the jacket ahead of her. Weaving through people, she felt the knocks as she went, her gaze remaining fixed on her target.

As she neared the person, she realized he was heading for the back exit. A voice in her head told her it would be stupid to follow, but if she didn't, she wouldn't know if it was actually *him*.

Squeezing through a couple more groups of people, Evie reached the door. Not thinking, she pushed through, finding herself standing in a deserted back parking lot. There were no people around, no chatter or music, just Evie and whoever was wearing that jacket.

A shiver worked its way up her spine as the chill in her bones intensified.

What was she thinking? She shouldn't be out here alone.

Turning back to the door, Evie wrapped her fingers around the handle. Her heart lurched when it didn't move. Locked.

Crap. This was not good.

A clattering noise from the right pulled her attention. Clenching her jaw, Evie took a step away from the door.

On her second step, laughter started from the same direction.

Double crap. Teeth now chattering, Evie froze on the spot.

Troy. It sounded just like Troy.

Her brain told her to run, but she couldn't get her legs to function. Evie knew she should scream, make noise, anything, but the connection between her brain and body seemed lost.

Then a shadow walked out from behind a tree. Evie's breath stopped. She could do nothing but stand and watch, a light-headed feeling coming over her.

Just as she was unsure whether her legs would keep her upright, the door behind her banged open. Turning her head, she saw Eden's large form walk through the doorway.

Spotting Evie, he gave her a once-over before glancing around the parking lot. A murderous look came over his face.

Evie took another step back, not sure who she should be more afraid of.

Keeping the door open with one foot, Eden reached for her arm with the other. Still frozen, she stumbled as he forced her feet to move. Placing Evie into the crook of his arm in a protective gesture, Eden glanced up and fixed his gaze on the very spot from which the laughter had emanated. The shadow of the man who had just been there, was now absent.

Keeping his gaze on that spot for a moment longer, Eden finally turned back to Evie.

"You okay?" The anger in his voice was still present, but it was softer than usual. Unsure how to react, she nodded before he continued. "Why are you out here?"

Clearing her throat, Evie forced her vocal cords to work. "I thought I saw someone I used to know." Her brows knitted together. Had she really seen him? Or was she just so fixated on the memory of the man, that she'd conjured up the jacket? It could have been the drinks... "I'm not sure I did," she mumbled, glancing back up at Eden.

For the first time since she'd met him, Evie felt relief at his presence, rather than dread. He was so big that Evie felt nothing could penetrate this guy's armor.

"Next time, bring one of us with you."

Nodding, Evie glanced around one last time but still saw nothing.

Moving her inside, Eden shut the door behind them. She stumbled a bit on her feet, and Eden frowned at her. "How much have you had to drink?"

Lifting a shoulder, Evie realized she didn't feel all that steady. "Not much."

Giving her another once-over, Eden gently took her upper arm and started heading toward Mason and Lexie.

Glancing down, Evie noticed she was still holding her drink. Throwing back her head, she downed the remainder. Lexie was right, she needed to relax.

As she followed Eden, she made a decision. Tonight was her

night off from being Evaline, victim of her ex and girl on the run. Tonight, she was just plain, twenty-six-year-old, Evie.

STEPPING INTO THE BAR, Luca did a quick scan before landing his gaze on Evie. His eyes narrowed when he saw guys dancing around her. Too damn close.

Done with caring about whether she thought they were in a relationship or not, he moved toward her.

He'd been at Marble doing the books with Asher when the call from Mason came through. Neither of them had hesitated. They just left.

Evie might see what they had as casual, but Luca knew it was anything but. The more time he spent with her, the more certain he was. She was his.

When he reached Evie, she had her back to him. He glared at the shaggy-haired asshole who was dancing with her.

Not hesitating, Luca placed a possessive arm around her waist and pulled her to his side.

Turning her head in surprise, Evie gasped. "Luca?"

"What the fuck, dude?" Shaggy Hair took a step closer. The guy was either stupid or drunk. Luca would put his money on both.

"You should go." Luca took his own step toward the guy, emphasizing their size difference.

For a moment, he seemed to contemplate a confrontation, then abruptly decided to reconsider and walk away. "Whatever."

Turning to face him, Evie stumbled. Luca caught her arm to steady her before pulling her against his chest. "Well, that was rude."

A hint of a smile touched Luca's lips. "Have you been drinking, Ms. Scott?"

Putting her hand on his chest, Evie attempted to push him

away. Luca remained where he was, but she did push herself back in the process. "I don't have to answer to you, Luca. I'm having a girl-free night."

Confused for a moment, he frowned. "Do you mean boy-free night?"

Pulling a face as if Luca was, in fact, the one who had said the wrong thing, Evie crossed her arms. "That's what I said."

Damn, she was cute.

Not giving it a second thought, Luca ran a hand up her back. A shiver coursed through her body when he lowered his mouth to her ear. "Dance with me."

A frown crossed her face. "I can't. Boy-free, and you smell good."

"Mmm, you smell good too. You feel even better. Dance with me, sweetheart."

"No." Even though she said the word, her whole body leaned into his, leaving barely any part of them not touching. "You're so big and warm. I could snuggle up to you every minute of every day."

A smile stretched Luca's lips. "Darling, you can snuggle up to this old body anytime you want."

Sighing, Evie rested her head on his chest. "I miss hugs. I don't get many hugs anymore."

Luca tightened his arms, every instinct telling him to keep this woman close. "I'll hug you anytime you want, Evie."

As they swayed to the music, he vaguely recognized that they were dancing much too slow for the upbeat tempo, but he wasn't complaining.

"I miss them, Luca."

Not sure what she meant, Luca glanced down at her. "Miss who?"

"My parents. You would have liked them. They were nice, like you." There was a slight pause before she continued. "You never know when it's going to be the last time you talk to someone. You think they'll always be there. More time."

Moving his hand in a slow circular motion on Evie's back, Luca lowered his voice. "I'm sorry."

Nodding against his chest, she sighed. "You guys are like family. Brothers. It's nice."

Knowing Evie was talking about the other guys at Marble Protection, Luca had to agree. "When you've been through as much together as we have, you become family."

"I wish I had a family."

The sadness in Evie's voice ate away at Luca. "Well, this family was formed on blood, sweat, and tears. Training was like being on the brink of death each day," Luca joked, trying to lighten the mood.

"Been there."

Stiffening, he stared at the top of Evie's head. "Been where, sweetheart?"

Ignoring his question, Evie continued, her words slurring slightly. "Maybe I didn't do enough to get away earlier? Like...I always thought I was the victim, but maybe it was my fault. Maybe I caused it all."

"You didn't." Luca's muscles clenched. His voice was firm, leaving no space for confusion. He didn't need her to explain to know the answer to that one.

"I wish I'd killed him. My life would be so much easier right now. That makes me a terrible person, doesn't it?" Insecurity leached into Evie's voice.

He lowered his mouth to her ear again. "No, it makes you human."

Head suddenly popping up, Evie frowned, her brows pulling together. "Trying not to like you is the most exhausting thing I've ever had to do, you know. Well, except for that day. That day was more exhausting."

Pushing a piece of hair behind her ear, Luca was starting to get lost in this conversation. "Which day?"

"The day I got away. The day the world went black. I'd almost given up hope. Almost accepted what was happening…but then I got out. And then the world went black."

Confused even more, Luca started to get a really bad feeling. "How did the world go black, Evie?"

Before she could answer, Lexie scooted up to them. "I'm gonna get going now, Asher's taking me home. Want a ride?"

Before Evie could respond, Luca did for her. "I've got it."

Raising her brows, she simply said, "Evie?"

Noticing Evie was now looking more tired than drunk, Luca wrapped his arm tighter around her waist.

"You guys made up. I knew you would."

Luca didn't try to understand what Evie was talking about, or the sappy look she was giving Lexie.

"Evie…ride?"

Shaking her head, she leaned further onto Luca. "I'll go with Luca. I've decided that tonight doesn't count."

Lexie's face softened. "I'm going to pretend to understand what you're talking about." Leaning close, she placed a kiss on Evie's cheek before turning to Luca. "Get her home safe."

With a nod, Luca watched her leave, Asher close on her tail.

"I'm tired, Luca."

Darting his gaze back down to Evie, he realized she was leaning on him heavily. Bending down, he wrapped his other arm around her legs as he scooped her up.

Instead of resisting, like he thought she would, Evie snuggled her head into his chest and closed her eyes. Walking out of the bar, he nodded at Mason and Eden on his way.

Evie slept the entire drive home, with Luca listening to her deep breaths. Once they arrived, instead of heading to her house, he carried her into his. When she woke, he'd make an excuse that he had better heating, but really, he just wanted her in his home. His bed.

Once inside, he moved up the stairs to his room, not even considering the guest bed. Gently placing Evie under the covers, he was about to head back downstairs when Evie's fingers touched his arm.

"Don't leave me, Luca."

Turning, Luca sat on the edge of the bed. Evie hadn't opened her eyes, but the sadness on her face was clear to see. "I won't, sweetheart, I'm just going to lock up and then I'll come back to bed."

"Promise. No matter what happens, promise you won't leave me. I've been so lonely and scared."

"I'm not going anywhere, sweetheart. And you won't be lonely or scared anymore. I promise."

With a soft sigh, Evie rolled over and fell back to sleep.

Watching her for a moment longer before moving away from the bed, Luca knew she was going to push him away again. It didn't matter, though. He wasn't going to let her go. That was a promise he intended to keep.

CHAPTER 14

*L*UCA EYED EVIE from across the lawn at the back of Marble Protection, the beer he held almost empty. She stood with Lexie, a smile curving her lips.

The team had decided to have a family barbecue to ease some of the pressure that had been building lately. They had been so caught up in finding everyone involved in Project Arma, they hadn't had time to stop and appreciate the fact they'd gotten out at all, let alone the business they'd built together.

Looking up, he noticed darker clouds were moving in, threatening rain, but so far, the weather was holding off.

Evie had woken up in his arms that morning, and Luca had every intention of making it a regular occurrence. She didn't seem to recall her drunk rambling from last night, or if she did, she hadn't mentioned it.

She'd admitted she was lonely and scared. He hated that. He hoped that his presence brought some level of calm into her life that hadn't been there before. Some added safety.

Looking over to Luca, Evie gave him a slow smile, her eyes softening. She was so damn beautiful—and she was *his*.

But he was a patient man. He could give her time.

"You guys get home okay last night?" Mason stepped up to Luca, holding out a fresh beer.

Taking it, he returned his attention to Evie. "Yeah, thanks for the call, buddy."

"Anytime." Mason's gaze scanned the lawn as he drank his own beer. "Did you get a chance to talk to Eden?"

Luca's grip tightened on the bottle at Eden's name. He'd been monitoring Eden's attitude toward Evie, and even though it had improved, it still wasn't where it needed to be.

"Haven't had a chance to talk today. Is there a reason you ask?" As Mason's eyes narrowed, Luca turned his full attention to his friend. "What is it?"

"There was someone there last night. Someone was watching Evie."

Luca's body tensed. "Who?"

"Didn't see his face."

"What the fuck do you mean, you didn't see his face? Did you go after him?" His voice rising, Luca attempted to tamp down the anger. The guys would be able to hear him regardless, but he didn't want to alert the women. Speaking in a quieter tone, Luca continued. "Tell me what happened."

"The girls showed up, so we watched them from a distance for a short while. Right after they arrived, a guy came in wearing a cap and a jacket. Wouldn't normally think anything of it, but the way he walked, Rocket…"

"What?"

Taking a moment before he continued, Mason's gaze moved from the yard to Luca. "He was like us."

Luca's fists clenched. "You're sure?"

"Yes."

How the fuck was this happening? Was some asshole from the facility after her? If so, it had to be because of him. *Fuck. Someone's following her because of me. I brought this to her door.*

"We thought that at first, too." Mason's expression didn't

change, but Luca knew he was about to tell him something else he wouldn't like. "We wanted to get to the girls quickly. Eden kept the guy in his sights. When we reached them, Evie saw the guy shortly after—and whoever he was, she recognized him."

Luca glanced over at Evie, his mind racing. "*Shit.*"

"She followed him outside." Luca's gaze swung back to Mason, and he almost shattered the glass bottle with his tense grip. "She locked herself out there with him by accident. Eden went out and found her. Whoever it was, Rocket, it wasn't someone she was happy to see. She was terrified."

"Then why the fuck did she follow him?"

Giving a shrug, Mason had a drink of his beer before he continued. "I think there are a few questions we should be asking her. We need answers."

Luca nodded. "Okay. Tomorrow, I'll chat with her." Knowing Mason was about to argue, Luca continued. "It can wait one more night. She must have her reasons for not sharing. It's not like I've shared all *my* secrets. Tonight's about family. She's safe here. It can wait."

The irritation was clear on Mason's face, but he didn't say anything further.

Needing to be closer to Evie, Luca headed to where she stood with Lexie. Placing a hand around her waist, he pulled her close.

"Well, if it isn't the knight in shining armor. I heard you indeed got my girl home safely last night. And by home, I mean *your* home." A smile on her face, Lexie moved her eyebrows up and down.

"In the future, I would appreciate an invite to these girls' nights."

With a laugh, Lexie placed a hand on her hip. "You're dreaming." Turning to Evie, she held up her drink. "Want another?"

When Evie shook her head, Lexie turned to leave.

Twisting Evie in his arms, Luca lowered his head before she had a chance to pull away. Her lips were so soft, making him want to deepen the kiss. Nibbling on her bottom lip, he pulled her body tighter against his. When she opened her mouth, Luca took advantage and eased his tongue inside.

Feeling himself hardening, he reluctantly pulled away. "You are too irresistible, Ms. Scott."

Smiling up at him, Evie had both hands on his chest, but this time, she didn't try to push him away. "How do you do that?"

"Do what?" Luca asked innocently.

"Make me feel like I can't get enough of you. Like I need more."

Luca's expression turned serious. He didn't want to sugar coat it. "Because nothing will *ever* be enough for you and me."

Looking a bit taken aback, Evie glanced down at her hands. "You say some really big things. I don't always know how to respond."

"I think direct is best with you."

A hint of a smile settled on Evie's face. "Guess I better stop pushing you away then."

Luca's own smile broke out. "She finally gets it."

Lowering his head to hers, Luca kissed her again, a calmness settling inside him.

LEAVING the group to head to the bathroom, Evie couldn't wipe the smile off her face. For the first time in a year, real hope bubbled inside of her that maybe her luck was changing. That maybe she and Luca would work out, and she could finally stop running.

This whole time she'd been trying to find a flaw in the guy, but so far, he seemed to be every bit the perfect guy she wanted to believe.

The bathroom was down the end of the hall, and the short

walk gave her time to reflect on the weekend. Was she just caught up in the moment, or could she really trust her feelings?

Evie had terrible instincts, but when she looked at Luca, she couldn't find any signs that warned her to stay away.

On her way back outside, Evie passed the office. Glancing inside, she stopped as something in the middle of the otherwise empty table caught her eye. Brows pulling together, she stood for a moment, undecided on whether to go in. Darting her gaze around to check that she was alone, she entered the room.

Halting just short of the table, Evie paused, nerves eating at her. She shouldn't be in here. If someone saw her snooping...if *Eden* saw her snooping... But something in her gut was telling her not to leave.

Moving closer, she saw a picture. Leaning down to pick it up, Evie's world stopped.

Fear almost swallowed her whole.

Those same hateful eyes that had tormented her for so long were staring into her own through the picture. His evil practically tore through the image and consumed her.

Dropping the picture as if it burned her fingers, Evie took a step back. Closing her eyes, she was bombarded by memories of the nightmare that was her life with Troy.

Taking several deep, shuddering breaths, she finally opened her eyes. Leaning down, she picked up the picture again with shaking fingers. Glancing at the other soldiers in the image, she saw what she'd missed the first time, her gaze so fixed on her ex.

Luca. Standing front and center. There was no denying it. Standing with him was Asher, Mason, Wyatt, Bodie, and Eden, as well as two other guys she didn't recognize.

Time stood still. *Luca knew Troy.* Luca completed *missions* with Troy; that seemed clear enough by the photo.

That had to mean that they were part of the same project. The project that poisoned good men. That ripped a man's soul from his chest and replaced it with ash.

The symbol on their vests caught her attention.

The Trident. Also known as the Budweiser to the men. Given to every person who successfully completed their SEAL training.

"No…"

Dropping the picture once again, Evie felt the room spin around her. This couldn't be happening. Luca could *not* be connected to such evil. Could he?

The evidence was right in front of her.

Did he know that man was *her* Troy? The Troy who had almost destroyed her? Was still trying to destroy her?

Maybe getting to know her was all one big ploy, and Troy was behind it? Oh God, did that mean Troy really *was* at her house? That she really *had* heard his laugh behind the bar?

Pivoting, she slammed her cold hand on the wall and took more deep breaths. The bile in her stomach began to rise, but she forced herself to calm down and think.

She had to get out. Not just out of Marble Protection, but out of Marble Falls.

How could she be so stupid? Trusting the wrong person had almost killed her once, and here she was, doing it again.

About to take off for the front door, she froze. She couldn't run. If she ran, Luca would know within minutes. She had to be smart. If she ran out now, he would follow. And he would catch her, there was no question about that.

Straightening her spine, breathing through her fear, Evie left the room. Walking back down the hallway, she forced her body to slow. She prayed that she could convince Luca she was okay.

Before she made it outside, Asher appeared in front of her. Her heart momentarily sped up before she consciously tried to settle it. Attempting to appear as normal as possible, Evie gave a small smile as she passed.

Asher's expression immediately changed, his brows drawing together. "Everything okay, Evie?" His hand lightly touched her arm. Evie wanted to shrink away, but used all her strength to remain still.

"Yeah, just not feeling well." Relieved that her voice sounded relatively calm, Evie tried to pass Asher, but his hand remained firm.

Taking a calming breath, she looked up into his eyes, seeing only concern.

"Anything I can help you with?"

"No. I'm okay. Thank you anyway, Asher." Darting her gaze away from his, she gave another quick smile before continuing down the hall, relieved when he finally removed his hand.

Heading back outside, Evie prayed that the agonizing fear wasn't showing on her face. Attempting a smile, she moved toward Luca.

Just like his friend's, Luca's expression also changed to one of concern. "You okay?"

Confidence knocked slightly, Evie dug her icy fingers into her palm to subdue the panic. "Luca, I'm not feeling too great. Might have been something I ate today. I'll just meet you at home."

Luca's hand reached out to touch her jaw, and she had to will her body not to flinch away. "Okay, I'll take you home."

"No," she said, too quickly. Calming her voice, Evie continued. "You stay. You were looking forward to this. I'll be fine, I just need to lie down for a bit."

Luca's eyes locked with Evie's, questioning. Searching. Her heart rate accelerated for a moment. Did he know she was running?

Just when she thought her heart would explode from her chest, a slight smile crossed his face.

"Okay, I'll see you at home." Pressing a soft kiss to her head, Luca lowered his mouth to her ear and uttered, "Stay safe, sweetheart."

Glancing up, Evie blinked tears away. He still felt like her Luca. The beautiful man who made her feel safe. Nurtured. Oh

God, she wished he was really the man she'd thought he was…but she couldn't get the image of him with Troy out of her head.

Anyone who was a part of Troy's life could not be part of hers.

Feeling too choked up to speak, Evie nodded before turning to leave. On her way out, she felt eyes on her but kept her gaze straight ahead. She had to get out. Now.

As soon as her feet hit the path outside Marble Protection, the first tear dropped. Scrubbing it away, Evie moved her legs faster. She'd let herself become too emotionally involved with the people at Marble Protection. But she had survived just fine on her own for the last ten months. She would survive now, too.

How had she not seen it? Luca had often seemed stronger than the average person, and so much faster. And his hearing… He could hear everything. She'd just refused to see it. Didn't *want* to see it. Wanted to believe there was good in most people. Safety in the man she'd fallen for.

How stupid was she? She hadn't learned a damn thing from Troy!

The only person who could keep her safe was herself.

Finally reaching her house, Evie's hand shook as she opened the front door. Walking into her room, memories of what they had shared in this space just two nights ago invaded her mind, and the tears fell harder. Evie didn't bother wiping them away.

Pulling the bag out from under her bed, Evie began throwing things in, taking only what she'd arrived with. As for money…she hadn't saved nearly enough.

Stopping, Evie closed her eyes and took a breath.

"You'll be okay. You'll work it out, and you'll survive like you always have." Opening her eyes, she tossed the last of the essentials into the bag before turning to leave.

Looking out the window first, Evie was relieved to see Luca hadn't changed his mind and returned home. With no sign of him or his car, she locked the door behind her. Moving to her car, she threw her bag in the back and slid in, putting her key in the ignition.

It wouldn't start.

Taking the key out of the ignition, Evie banged her fist on the steering wheel out of frustration, then dropped her head back on the headrest.

You're okay, Evie. You've got this. You got away once, you'll get away again.

The difference was that she had dreamed about escaping Troy. Escaping the fists and the abuse. This time, she was running from a man who had shown her kindness. The man who had crept his way into her heart and filled a spot that had been hollow for years.

Evie straightened, a new determination filling her.

Putting her key in the ignition again, Evie tried starting the car a few more times. On what felt like the tenth try, the engine turned over. Backing the car out of the driveway with a sigh of relief, Evie gave one last look at Luca's house before turning away.

Just look forward, Evie. Everything will be okay.

The farther she drove, the more her chest hurt.

Evie glanced back to see a car enter her rearview mirror. As it got closer, her heart stuttered.

Luca. It was his car, clear as day, trailing behind her.

Pressing her foot on the accelerator, Evie tried to push the car harder. As she sped up, so did Luca. Though he only sped enough to keep her in his sights, never getting too close.

As she picked up speed, a red light on the dashboard started blinking. Dread filled her chest. Her car wasn't going to make it. It could barely cope with *normal* speeds.

Come on, Honda.

A moment later, smoke started billowing from the hood of the car. After a loud bang from the engine, startling Evie, the car slowed of its own volition.

Looking back, Evie saw Luca was almost upon her.

Making a split-second decision, she slammed her foot on the brake. Having completely forgotten her seat belt, she hit the steering wheel hard. Ignoring the pain, Evie jumped out of the car and dashed toward the forest.

She couldn't outrun him. There was no way. But with a head start, maybe she could hide before he got to her. What other choice did she have?

Pushing her legs to move, Evie raced through the trees. The memory of the last time she did this very same thing screamed through her mind. A sob tore from her chest. She had to focus on placing one foot in front of the other. She needed to keep moving.

The branches scratching at her arms and face didn't register. Neither did the cold wind or the tightness in her chest.

She had one goal: hide.

As Evie ran, the skies opened, and the heavens doused her in buckets of rain. It was like the sky was bleeding.

At the sound of rustling behind her, she choked down another sob. Veering toward the closest big tree, Evie dropped to the ground behind it and focused on silencing her breaths and slowing her heartbeat.

CHAPTER 15

*S*LOWING THE CAR, Luca kept a safe distance from Evie. His concern for her went through the roof when she accelerated at the sight of him. She needed to slow down too. Her car wasn't in good enough condition to drive so fast.

When Evie returned from the bathroom at Marble Protection, she'd not been herself, a suspicion she confirmed by deciding to leave. Luca had wanted to insist on going with her, but one look at her face and he knew that if he did, he wouldn't find out what was wrong.

She'd worn a closed-off expression. The same one on her face when he'd first met her.

Something had happened during Evie's short trip inside the building, and Luca was going to find out what.

A few minutes after she'd left Marble Protection, Asher came outside and walked up to Luca, holding a picture.

"I spotted Evie coming out of the office. This was on the floor."

Taking the picture from Asher's fingers, Luca noted it was the image of his team, with the other SEAL unit behind them.

Passing the picture back to Asher, Luca hadn't known what

the hell was going on, but he'd already started walking. "I'm going after her."

The team watched him leave. No one stopped him because they all wanted answers.

A curse escaped Luca's lips at the sight of smoke coming from Evie's car. Her vehicle abruptly veered to the side of the road, coming to a sudden stop, forcing Luca to slam on his brakes or shoot past her.

Then he watched as Evie abruptly opened her car door and raced into the trees.

Goddammit.

Coming to a stop behind Evie's car, Luca wasted no time going after her. Tuning into his surrounding, he could hear her heavy steps and frantic breathing.

Pumping his legs and using his SEAL training, he followed her trail through the trees. He ignored the sound of the birds and the wind, focusing solely on her. Quieting his steps as much as possible, he heard Evie drop to the ground.

Forcing himself to slow, Luca moved toward the tree where the sound had emanated, making sure she wouldn't hear him until the last moment.

Quickly moving around the tree, he saw Evie crouched on the ground. Terror shone in her eyes.

What the hell?

Jumping to her feet, Evie tried to run but tripped over a tree root on her third step. Luca's arm shot out to catch her before she could fall.

Not anticipating her lifting her feet and kicking out, he tightened his grip and dropped to the wet ground, ensuring his body took the impact before rolling and pinning her beneath him.

Evie kept flailing, her breaths becoming shorter and her heart rate increasing, both loud despite the pounding rain.

"Evie, stop!"

Ignoring him, she slipped her bent legs between them and tried to thrust out, kicking him away.

Using his feet to pin her legs, Luca dropped his hips, effectively shackling her to the ground. Raising his voice, Luca repeated, "Evie, stop now."

With a sob, Evie shouted, "Get off me! I want to go."

Confusion filled him. Studying her face, he racked his brain for any answer to what was going on. "Go where?"

"Away."

Frustration welled. "Why?"

"I just want to go! Please!"

The desperation in her voice almost undid him. Almost. "I need you to tell me why, sweetheart."

In the pregnant silence, a lone tear slid from her eye, lost in the rain soaking them both.

Taking a chance, he let go of her left hand and brushed her temple gently, where the tear had fallen. "Was there something about that picture in the office that upset you?"

Swinging her gaze back to his, fresh terror entered Evie's eyes, but still she said nothing.

"Please, Evie. I want to understand."

Evie's indecision was clear to see, before she spoke quietly. "It was *him*."

Confused, Luca frowned. "Who?"

Evie was silent for a moment before uttering a name Luca had never expected. "Troy."

Even with all his training, he struggled to keep the surprise off his face. "You know Troy?"

Fury filled Evie's expression, but no further words left her.

Then it hit him. Troy was the ex. The ex that she was running from.

Evie was running from the same man his team was trying to find. "You were dating *Troy*?" Even as he said the words, they didn't make sense in his mouth.

"Yes."

Luca felt like he'd been sucker-punched. How was this possible? "And he's the one who hurt you?"

He wanted her to say no. But when her nod answered his question, it took all his strength not to reveal the anger coursing through his veins.

That asshole had touched her. *Hurt* her.

"Please just let me get out of town. I promise I'll stay away!"

Understanding dawned on him. "You ran because you think Troy and I are friends?"

The silence that followed was all the confirmation Luca needed. He tried to push down the hurt that Evie would assume he was anything like that asshole. All this time, he thought he'd been building trust with her. Showing her that he was different. Had it meant nothing to her?

"We weren't part of the same team, and we've certainly never been friends, Evie."

"But the picture—"

"SEALs go on the same missions sometimes. I barely knew the guy."

Hope entered Evie's expression before she quickly masked it. "Even if that's true, I can't be a part of anything he's touched."

Even if? What would it take for this woman to believe him? Trust him?

Then another thought occurred to him. Did she know what they could do? What was done to them at Project Arma?

"Why can't you be part of anything that he touched?"

The sorrow that washed over her face made Luca want to wrap his arms around her and protect her from the entire world.

"Because I can't make another mistake that I'll live to regret." Her words were quiet.

"Tell me what you regret, Evie."

Her voice bled with the pain and anger he knew she was drowning in. "Everything! I regret dating that asshole and falling for his lies. I regret trusting him. I regret letting him hurt me. But mostly I regret giving up. I got so tired, and I gave up fighting for myself. When someone treats you like shit for long enough, you start believing you're as worthless as they say."

"I'm so sorry, sweetheart."

Shaking her head, Evie continued. "And because of him, my parents are dead. He murdered them, Luca! I can't prove it, but I *know* he did. They probably started asking too many questions. Raising too many red flags. They were good people. He could do whatever he wanted to me, but my parents didn't deserve that! When they died, it felt like my heart was ripped from my chest. He left me with *nothing*. I was weak, but I'll never be weak again."

That son of a bitch. Luca would kill him. Tear him apart with his bare hands.

But right now, Luca needed to keep her talking. He needed more answers. As the rain came down heavier, he pushed down his anger and asked his next question. "So, you've been running and hiding since you got away?"

Evie nodded. "I can't let him find me."

"He won't. I won't let him."

"You can't stop him, Luca! No one can."

Speculation grew. "Why do you think no one can stop him?"

Evie chewed her bottom lip. Her lips were turning purple from the cold rain that soaked their clothes, causing them to stick to their skin. His body sheltered her from the worst of the weather, but there was no stopping the wind.

"Once Troy decides something, that's it."

As her teeth began to chatter, Luca decided it was time to get to shelter.

Slowly standing, he took Evie's arms and pulled her up with him. "Let's go home, sweetheart, and get warm. Then you can tell me more."

Shaking her head, Evie tried to wrench her arm away. Luca let her, not wanting her to hurt herself. "I want to leave."

He couldn't allow that. He didn't just need answers—he needed Evie. There was no way he was going to let her walk away and disappear from his life. Not when he could protect her. "Can you afford to leave right now?"

The doubt in Evie's eyes said what she didn't.

"Stay. You have a job, a roof over your head, and my friends and I will look out for you."

A bitter laugh broke from Evie's chest as her arms wrapped around her waist. "They hate me."

"They'll look after you." As the rain fell harder, his urgency to get to shelter grew. "And they don't hate you. They just have a hard time trusting."

Shivers racked her body. "I *will* leave, Luca. I always do."

Luca's heart splintered. Was he fighting a losing battle?

Taking Evie's hand, he was relieved when she didn't pull away again. As they headed back to their cars, he strategically positioned his body to block most of the wind. "I'll send one of the guys to fix your car and bring it home."

Without a word, Evie got into Luca's vehicle and buckled her seat belt. Luca quickly grabbed the bag he spotted in her backseat before joining her.

The drive home was silent. Luca cranked the heater as high as it went and kept Evie in his peripheral vision, relieved when her shaking subsided.

Parking his car in his driveway, Luca glanced at Evie. Even drenched from head to toe and red-faced from crying, she was still the most beautiful woman he'd ever seen.

After a few moments, she broke the silence. "You really weren't friends with him?"

Luca didn't hesitate. "Not even close, sweetheart."

Looking up at the sky through the front windscreen, Evie seemed to contemplate his words. "He wasn't always a bad guy," she finally said. "When we first started dating, he was good... kind. Sweet even. He would hold doors for me. Kiss me goodbye on the cheek." A shadow crossed Evie's face. "Then…he changed. I don't know why, but he did."

"Tell me about him." Luca hadn't known Troy pre-Project Arma, and the man he *had* known was never good.

Evie wrung her hands. Luca had already identified it as a nervous trait. "We started dating in senior year. He went off to join the Navy. Then a few years into our relationship, he asked me to move to the country with him. I jumped at the idea. Stupid. I was young and thought I loved the guy. He was away so often on missions, so I thought living with him would bring us closer together. At first, it wasn't so bad. But pretty soon, I started to realize how isolated I was. No job, no friends. I didn't even have a car."

Pausing, Evie closed her eyes for a moment. "The changes started with him losing his temper every so often. He would throw things, break stuff. At first, he would always apologize after. By the end, he was angry *all* the time. When he didn't get his way, he would explode. You didn't want to be around him when that happened. When he started taking his anger out on *me*…by that stage, I didn't have contact with anyone except my parents. When it started getting bad, I contacted them less and less. I couldn't get away. I was stuck. Alone."

"I'm sorry."

"Don't say sorry, Luca. I don't deserve it. I shouldn't have put myself into a position where I was helpless. And I won't ever again."

Covering her small hand with his larger one, Luca leaned closer. "It's okay to let people help you, Evie."

She remained quiet for a moment, her expression turning thoughtful. "I guess. I mean…I keep pushing *you* away, but you keep sticking around."

Because there was no question for him. She was it. "You're worth fighting for."

Shaking her head, Evie turned away to stare out her window.

"I don't *feel* worth fighting for. I feel like he stripped me of every inch of self-worth that I possessed."

Luca's heart broke for the beautiful woman sitting next to him. "You have a right to feel damaged, Evie, but don't confuse damage with destruction."

Turning to face him, Evie placed her hand on his cheek. "I'm glad you keep coming back to me, Luca." Leaning over, she placed a kiss on his cheek before exiting the car.

Watching her walk away, Luca finally allowed the rage to take over. Troy was trying to destroy Evie. Had already hurt her. Killed her family.

A deadly determination filled him. Evie would feel safe. And he would make damn sure Troy got what he deserved for everything he'd done.

CHAPTER 16

*N*ERVOUS TENSION RADIATED through Evie as she drove to Marble Protection.

It was the day after she'd tried to run, and the knowledge that all the guys now knew she'd dated Troy made her want to run under the nearest rock and hide. She knew Luca had already explained some of her past to them, but they didn't have the blind faith in Evie that he did.

There was also the fact that she now suspected what they were capable of. What they had been turned into: machines.

Being Navy SEALs, they'd already been the best of the best, but now that she knew they could do everything Troy could do, they weren't just dangerous. They would be unstoppable.

Evie hadn't told Luca everything last night. In particular, she hadn't mentioned that she knew he was probably just as deadly as Troy.

She wanted to trust him. Oh God, did she want to. But there was a huge block there. Something that said trusting anyone with all her secrets was like standing at the edge of a cliff and inviting them to push you off.

Maybe Troy *had* broken her. Maybe Evie would never trust

another soul again. But the thought of a life without Luca felt empty, and that scared the hell out of her. She knew she needed to make a decision on whether to trust him and let him in completely, or stay away, but either option filled her with paralyzing fear.

Entering the building, Evie didn't make it to the desk before she was hit full force by Lexie, who wrapped her arms around Evie in a tight bear hug.

"Holy mother of pearl, girl. You scared the crap out of me!" Lexie exclaimed, pulling out of the hug but keeping her hands on Evie's shoulders. "You leave the party with no warning and no goodbye. The guys tell me you're sick. Then I can't reach you. What the heck? Ever heard of friendship etiquette?"

Evie squirmed under Lexie's intense stare, hating that she had to lie to her friend. "I'm sorry. I think I just ate something that didn't agree with me. I'm feeling a lot better today."

With a single raised brow, Lexie's expression said she didn't believe her. "Is that the truth?"

Technically, Evie *had* felt sick, just not because of something she'd eaten. "Mostly."

"Girl, you have too many secrets. I'd stay and hound you, but I know you'll share when you're ready. Plus, this girl needs some new shoes."

With a relieved laugh, Evie walked around Lexie and stepped behind the desk. "I thought this was a 'no spend' month."

With a pout, Lexie put a hand to her chest. "Do you have no faith in me? With the sales I intend to find, I'll be *saving* money." Flinging her bag on her shoulder, she headed toward the door before turning back. "Next time, say goodbye, okay? There are people here who care about you."

Feeling guilty, Evie simply nodded. Once Lexie was gone, she got to work.

Throughout the day, she saw the guys come and go. Most smiled at her. Asher even stopped for a chat. Bodie asked how she was going. They acted like nothing had happened, and for that, she was grateful.

Apart from seeing Luca when she left the house that morning, she hadn't seen him all day. She tried not to think of him, but he kept popping into her thoughts anyway. It was like the guy was tattooed on her eyeballs.

By the end of the day, it was just her and Eden in the building. Something had changed between them since the night at the bar. She still wouldn't be sending the guy a Christmas card, but at least she didn't feel the need to cower behind the desk every time he was around.

Shutting down the computer, Evie startled when she looked up to see Eden on the other side of the desk.

Jeez, these guys need to wear a bell or something.

"I'll be back in a sec, don't leave until I return, okay?"

Evie nodded, confused about what was going on. But before she could blink, he was out the front door.

That was strange.

Evie watched him leave, wondering where he was going. And why did she have to wait for him to get back? It was getting dark outside, but it wasn't like she hadn't walked home at this time by herself before.

Still, better to listen to Eden than deal with his wrath later. He was being nicer to her now, and she didn't want to risk the old Eden showing his face.

Tapping the desk with her fingers, Evie glanced around, wondering what to do while she waited. Spotting the cleaning supplies cupboard, she grabbed some spray and wipes. If she was going to stay, she might as well do something productive. Moving around the desk, she started with the gym area.

As she began wiping the equipment, a noise from the entrance drew her attention. Thinking it might be Eden, Evie stood, but when she glanced at the front, there was no one there.

A nervous tingle climbed up her spine.

Moving back to the counter, she rummaged through her purse and retrieved her phone. Feeling slightly safer with it in her hands, she turned it on. On the first day at work, Luca had entered his number into her phone, but she'd never called it. Luca had always called *her*.

As another creak echoed through the silent room, Evie searched the phone for his number. Agitation racked her body as her fingers hovered over his name.

She couldn't shake the feeling that something wasn't right. Was she just being paranoid? Overreacting because of her past?

As she started to put down the phone, the room suddenly darkened, all the lights going out.

Her trepidation intensified, and Evie's clammy hands shook as they hit dial.

He picked up on the first ring, and Evie let out a sigh of relief.

"Evie?" Luca sounded surprised. Just hearing his deep gravelly voice steadied her slightly.

"Um, hey," she muttered. Now that he was on the line, she felt silly.

"What's wrong?"

Hearing the concern in his tone, Evie chided herself for calling him unnecessarily. What was she doing? She must be losing her mind.

"Nothing, I shouldn't have called," she said. Nibbling her lip, Evie went with the truth. "I'm waiting for Eden at the gym, and the lights suddenly went out. It's nothing. I shouldn't have called."

"Where's Eden?" Luca's response was immediate.

"Um, I'm not sure. He popped out and told me to wait for—" Before Evie could finish, a shuffling noise in the corner of the room made her pause. The hairs on her arms stood up and her muscles froze.

As if sensing that she wasn't okay, Luca's voice came through the line again. "Stay where you are, Evie. I'm coming now. Stay on the line for me, okay, sweetheart?"

Before she could respond, Evie cried out when she was grabbed from behind. Brutal fingers wrapped around her neck and forced her onto her toes.

The phone dropped from her fingers as she desperately grabbed at the hands preventing breath from entering her body.

Trying to suck in air, she felt as if her throat was glued shut. Black dots entered her vision as she drifted toward unconsciousness.

The fingers around her throat abruptly released before she passed out. Then the hands grabbed her from behind and flung her through the air. She hit the wall, hard.

Gasping, Evie felt a ruthless boot kick her in the face, then the ribs. Pain radiated throughout her body. Already she felt the throbbing and swelling in her cheek. She wouldn't be surprised if a rib was fractured.

A firm hand slammed her head to the floor, causing agony to shoot through her skull. She prayed for it to stop.

Hot breath touched her ear. "Tell lover boy I'm coming for him. Then I'm coming for you."

At the sound of his voice, the pain faded into nothingness, replaced by fear. It was so intense that her body froze in the fetal position, a whimper escaping her lips.

He was here. In the same room. Touching her.

"I'm glad you get it, Evaline."

The hand remained on her head for another moment and she felt his face nuzzle her hair, before he slammed her to the floor one last time and stood. Another kick landed on her ribs.

Letting out another cry, Evie heard footsteps retreat before the room went silent.

Lying against the wall, she vaguely recognized that her breaths didn't sound right. There was a crackling in her chest that shouldn't be there. Something was broken.

As darkness started to work its way into her vision, she heard the subtle sound of footsteps again. *Please don't let it be him.*

She couldn't take any more.

Hands touched the uninjured side of her face. Rather than the violence and coldness of the hands that had just been on her, these were soft. Gentle. It had to be Eden or Luca...

That's good. At least if she was going to pass out, or worse, she wouldn't be alone. Evie hated being alone.

CHAPTER 17

"WHAT THE FUCK happened?" Luca shouted, shoving Eden against the hospital wall. The guy had a couple inches on him, but Luca was just as deadly, and he had rage on his side.

All the guys stood in the hospital hallway except Asher, who guarded Evie inside her room. They weren't taking any chances.

"Get off me, Rocket." Even though he made the demand, Eden didn't attempt to defend himself or push Luca away.

Grabbing his friend's shirt, Luca pulled him forward, only to shove him back against the wall again. Frustration ate at him and he was nearing the end of his patience. "Why weren't you there to protect her like you were supposed to be?"

Eden's expression didn't change. "There was someone outside."

Luca paused. "What the hell are you talking about?"

"Someone was staking out Marble Protection. I noticed about an hour before I left to check it out." Luca stepped back. "I thought Evie was safe, seeing as I was tracking the guy. I followed the tracks, but when I got down the street, I heard Evie shout and went back. I was too late. The guy who attacked her was gone."

Running his hands through his hair, Eden leaned against the wall. "I should have stayed to protect her, and I didn't."

The only thing stopping Luca from beating his friend's ass was that he already looked like hell. Worry glazed his eyes and the veins in his arms bulged like he wanted to murder someone. As he damn well should.

"How did he get away so easily?" Mason questioned, stepping forward.

He voiced the question everyone was thinking. She should have been safe. Just one of them was the equivalent of a team of regular soldiers guarding her.

"That's what I want to know," Eden said, rage filling his voice.

From his place against the opposite wall, Wyatt spoke up. "There could have been two of them."

"No, there was one guy," Eden responded, fists clenched. "Don't ask me how I know, but I do, and when I find him, I'm going to murder the fucker."

"Not if I do first." Running his hands through his hair, Luca was only just keeping his fury in check. "Troy. It's Troy. I know it."

No one said anything. There was nothing they *could* say. Everyone knew he was the most likely culprit.

Mason lowered his voice slightly. "I know you probably don't want to hear this, man, but that might be a good thing. We've been searching for him and his team for a damn year and have found nothing on our own."

Luca's blood boiled. Was he serious? Evie lay in a goddamn hospital bed, and Mason thought this was a good thing?

With a quiet but deadly tone, Luca barely restrained himself. "A good thing? Evie's not *bait*. That asshole could have killed her."

Placing his hands in the air, Mason moved back half a step. "I wasn't saying she is, Rocket. We're all gonna stick to her day and night. You know nothing else will happen to her from here on out. If that jerk's around, we'll get him."

Trying to calm the turmoil inside him, Luca shook his head as his eyes rose to the ceiling. "I hate this. I fucking *hate* it! I should have been there."

How had he let this happen? He knew someone had been in her house, knew they were followed in the woods...and still, he let her out of his sight.

Walking forward, Luca opened the door to her room. "I'm staying with her tonight." Not waiting for a response, he stepped inside. As he turned, his breath hitched. She looked so small and fragile in the bed.

The left side of her face was a mixture of blacks and purples from where she'd been kicked, and he knew she also had three cracked ribs. One fracture just missed puncturing her lung.

Before he could take a step closer, Asher rose from the chair. "How you doing, buddy?" The concern in his friend's voice was clear.

"Like one half of me wants to stick to her like glue, and the other half wants to go out and search for the fucker and rip him apart."

And that was the honest truth. It was like his mind was at war. For now, he knew he needed to be with her. Soon though, he would get the guy who did this.

Walking forward, Luca stopped at Asher's hand on his arm.

"There's something else. While I was in here, I checked her chart. The doc found evidence of a shitload of past trauma. Broken ribs, fractured wrists, ankles. Her record of past injuries looks like a damn shopping list."

Luca clenched his fists. The taste of acid filled his mouth at the thought of what Evie had been through at Troy's hands.

"We'll find him, Rocket."

"Damn straight." Without another word, he pulled the chair to the side of the bed. He heard the door open, but he only had eyes for Evie. Gently wrapping his fingers around her hand, Luca pressed his lips to her wrist. Listening to her heartbeat and knowing she was alive calmed him somewhat.

"I'm sorry, sweetheart. I should have been there. I shouldn't have left you."

Luca remained in the chair for what felt like minutes, his mind raging, but it was actually hours before he felt the twitch of her hand.

Glancing up, he watched as Evie's eyes opened. She glanced around for a moment before fixing on him, a small frown on her face.

"Luca?"

"Yeah, darlin', it's me." He placed a kiss on her hand, his thumb gently stroking her wrist.

Trying to sit up, Evie grimaced.

Placing his hands on her shoulders, Luca slowly eased her back onto the pillows. "You need to rest. Don't worry, I'm not leaving your side."

Lying down, Evie closed her eyes. Instead of sadness, anger washed over her face. "It was him." It was a statement, not a question.

"Doesn't matter who it was. He won't get near you again."

"I want to believe you. I really do. But you don't know Troy." She opened her eyes, a mixture of anger and contempt shining through. "I want to kill him, Luca. I don't care if that makes me a bad person. He thinks he has the right to touch me, to hurt me, but he doesn't."

"You're right. He doesn't have the right to touch you, and he never will again." So damn proud of her strength, Luca squeezed her shoulder. "And I *do* know Troy, Evie, but even if I didn't, the guys and I won't let anything else happen to you."

Turning her head toward the window, she said quietly, "You know, the more I think about it, the more I think I did everything wrong."

"What do you mean, sweetheart?"

"When things got bad in the end, I had to secretly call my parents when he wasn't around. They were planning to come and save me. We had it all worked out. Then one day, he disconnected the land line. After that, he rarely left the house. One of the few times he did, he forgot his cellphone, so I called them. A girl answered. When I asked where my parents were, she told me the previous owners had died in a home invasion about a month earlier.

"When Troy got home, he could tell something was off with me. I told him what happened. He laughed and told me to get over it."

Turning her gaze back to Luca, Evie spoke with an uncontained rage. "My parents had been dead for a *month*, and I didn't even know. I let it break me. I ran like a coward. I should have used it as fuel to devise a plan to end *him*. Instead, I've been wasting my life running."

Damn, this woman had to be the strongest person he'd ever met.

"Escaping when faced with someone with Troy's training was smart, Evie. Running gave you time. Time to try to heal and to make a plan. Now you have the guys and me."

"I don't want him hurting people I care about again, Luca. And I don't want to have to rely on other people to save me."

Gripping her hand tighter, Luca spoke in a firm voice. "You don't worry about me, Evie. The guys and I are more than capable of taking care of ourselves. And you've been doing everything yourself for too damn long. Maybe it's time to let someone help you."

Looking unconvinced, Evie nodded absently. "He said something before he left. He said he's coming for you."

Luca's eyes narrowed. "Let him." He meant it. He welcomed Troy coming after him. It would save him the search because, from this point on, he did intend to scour the earth. If Troy came after him, Luca could kill the guy that much sooner.

With a sigh, Evie's eyes fluttered shut. As silence descended, Luca watched her chest rise and fall.

"I wish I'd met you first."

Her words were no louder than a whisper, but she may as well have yelled; they were so clear. They tore at Luca's heart.

Leaning down, he pressed a kiss to Evie's forehead. "You've met me now, and I'm not going anywhere. Rest, sweetheart. I'm not leaving the hospital. You're safe."

He waited until her breath evened out before sending a text to the team to come in. Once they were all in the room, Asher spoke first.

"How is she?"

"Physically, she'll heal. Mentally and emotionally, not so great. But she's a fighter, and she has me. I'm going to make sure she's okay." Standing, Luca faced the team. These were the men that he trusted with his life. He needed their support now. "I'm staying here tonight." The words didn't leave any room for argument.

Asher nodded. "Roger that. Eagle and I will go to Marble Protection and see if we can find anything important."

Wyatt reached into his pocket to grab his keys. "I'll hack the security footage of the surrounding areas and see what I can learn."

Eden hadn't taken his eyes from Evie. "I'll guard the hospital hallway tonight." He glanced at Luca, his eyes filled with guilt. "I've been distracted, Rocket, and I'm sorry, but I won't let you down again."

Giving him a nod of acknowledgment, Luca was glad to see a glimpse of his old friend. He was grateful to have the support of his brothers when he needed them most.

Luca finally released a breath he hadn't realized he'd been holding.

"Cage and Ax are returning from their missions. They haven't had much luck in locating the scientists, so when we told them what was going on, they were keen to get back," Bodie said.

"It'll be good to have their support," Luca agreed as he sat back down next to Evie. "When she's released, I'm going to take her to my place. I'm not leaving her side again."

Asher squeezed Luca's shoulder. "Take care, man."

They filtered out, leaving Luca with a sleeping Evie and his tormented thoughts.

CHAPTER 18

*E*VIE FELT LIKE she'd been hit by a truck. Rolling over, pain radiated through her ribs, causing a grimace. Letting out a small groan, she wrapped her arms around her middle.

When the bedroom door opened, she shot up into a sitting position, air whooshing out of her. A new round of pain hit and Luca was by her side in an instant.

"Jeez, Evie, be careful! Are you okay?"

Grabbing his arm, she tried to take some deep breaths before looking up. "I'm okay." Glancing around for the first time, she realized they weren't in her house. "I'm in your room."

A hint of a smile touched Luca's lips. "That's correct."

Swinging her gaze back to him, Evie cocked her head in question.

"Come on, my place has central heating and cooling, no holes in the wall, plus a king-size bed. You can't beat that."

Well, the bed *was* comfy. Plus, it smelled like Luca.

"Okay, but if you see Misty, can you feed her?"

The confusion on his face almost made her laugh. "Misty?"

"She's a cat that's been coming over. She's always hungry so I feed her." And pat her. And cuddle her. Evie leaned back against the pillows. "I feel like I could sleep all day."

Sitting beside her, Luca pressed a kiss to Evie's forehead. "Then that's what you should do."

Just as she closed her eyes, the sound of banging on the front door had them popping open again.

"Stay here, I'll check who it is."

Feeling nervous tension return to her shoulders, Evie painfully pushed herself into a sitting position. She didn't have to wonder who it was for long, as a hysterical woman's voice sounded from downstairs, followed by loud footsteps.

Before Evie could blink, Lexie plowed through the bedroom door. With tears building in her eyes, she froze for a moment at the sight of Evie, unmoving.

Jeez, she must look worse than she thought.

"Oh my God, are you okay?" Walking over, she sat carefully on the edge of the bed. "I want to give you a hug, but I don't want to hurt you."

Leaning forward, Evie slowly wrapped her arms around Lexie. She felt the twinge of pain, but it was worth it. Lexie gently hugged her back.

Only a month ago, she'd felt lost and alone. Survival was the only thing she could spare any thought for. Now, having people who cared made Evie want to hold them tight and never let go. Reluctantly pulling back when her ribs protested, Evie eased to the pillows once more.

"Thanks for coming, Lex. I'm okay, a few fractured ribs and some bruises. Everything will heal."

Placing a hand on Evie's uninjured cheek, Lexie leaned close. "You're such a strong woman. I can't imagine what you went through last night."

Shrugging, Evie dropped her gaze. "It's nothing I haven't experienced before."

Lexie released a gasp, her eyes widening. "Someone's hurt you like this before?"

Deciding it was time to trust her friend, Evie nodded. "My ex. We were together for years. He was a good man at the start. Now...I don't even know *what* he is. At some point, he changed. So I ran and...here I am."

"No!" Tears fell from Lexie's eyes. "I'm so sorry that happened to you, Evie. Is he out of your life now?"

Evie paused before answering. "Actually, he's the one who did this."

This time, Lexie's eyes looked like they were going to bug out of her head. If the situation wasn't what it was, Evie might have actually laughed.

"*Why?*"

Wasn't that the magic question? "I don't know. Since I got away, I've had plenty of time to think about it. I guess maybe he saw me as his property or something, and he's pissed I got away from him."

Shaking her head, Lexie placed a hand on Evie's knee. "I'm glad you're here now. You ran to the right place. If anyone can protect you, it's Luca and the guys." Noticing the hesitation in Evie's eyes, Lexie frowned. "What? You're not still unsure about Luca, are you? The guy is infatuated with you, Evie! God, he's beside himself right now with worry."

Fiddling with the blanket, Evie glanced down. "I know. I don't deserve him."

"Evie Scott, look at me." At Lexie's stern voice, Evie glanced back up. "Find your damn courage, girl. There's a brave woman inside of you, and she's fucking brilliant. Got it? Don't let some asshole make you think otherwise. You're deserving of love and a future, and so is Luca. Believe in what you've found and have faith."

Hadn't Evie tried to tell herself something similar about a hundred times? Making herself believe it was another thing entirely. "I want to, Lexie, I really do, but trusting another guy feels like the scariest thing in the world."

"I know. But if you care about someone, trust them. *Tell* them that you care, Evie. Even if it scares the shit out of you." Pain flashed through Lexie's eyes. "If I had what you and Luca have, I wouldn't question it for a second."

Heart softening, Evie took Lexie's hand. "I'm sorry if things haven't been working out with Asher." She frowned. "I know I always seem to have a million things going on, but you can talk to me, Lex. I want to be there for you too."

Shaking her head, Lexie gave her a smile that didn't quite reach her eyes. "Thank you, sweetie, but it's nothing. I swear."

Evie knew that smile. She'd perfected it over the years. It was the smile meant to mask the pain, but it rarely worked. Evie wanted to push, but she knew from ample experience that a person would share when they were ready.

Standing, Lexie gave Evie a soft hug. "I need to get to work. I just had to check on you first. I'm going to come back after my shift. What can I bring for you? Soup? Comfort bear? Peanut butter M&M's with a side of Twinkies?"

Even though it hurt, Evie couldn't stop the laugh from escaping. "I'm okay, Lex. Just seeing you is like medicine."

Lexie gave another small smile. "Okay, but call if you need anything. Promise?"

"Promise."

With a nod, Lexie turned and left. Then Evie was alone again.

For the first time, she really studied Luca's room, noticing how clean it was. Everything seemed to have a place. It was masculine, too, the color palette a mixture of grays and blues. The bed she lay in was huge—much bigger than her own double bed, and softer, too. She felt like she could melt into the satin sheets.

As the bedroom door opened, Evie's gaze swung around to

meet Luca's. He looked big and fearless, like no one could ever break him.

"How are you feeling, sweetheart?"

"Like I've been kicked in the face." Evie cracked a small smile while Luca's expression turned steely. "Sorry."

Walking into the room, he handed Evie a glass with some pills. "Pain meds."

She put both on the nightstand. "I don't need them, Luca, but thank you."

Reaching over, Luca picked them right back up. "You have to take your pain meds, Evie. Doctor's orders."

Rolling her eyes, she put her hands in her lap. "I've been through this before and never bothered with pain meds."

At Luca's distraught expression, Evie immediately wished she could take back the words. Grabbing the pills and water, she swallowed the medication and lay back on the pillow. "Will you lie with me until I fall asleep?"

Features softening, Luca walked around the bed and got under the covers. Placing her head on his shoulder, Evie closed her eyes and let the cocoon of Luca's arms lull her to sleep.

With silent steps, Evie crept into the office. Troy had left the door unlocked for the first time. She was a prisoner in this house and couldn't even access every room.

He was outside, and she knew he'd be back quickly. She had only minutes to find out what she could.

Heart thundering, she moved toward the open laptop on the desk. If she got caught, the consequences could be deadly, but she needed to know.

Did his laptop hold any answers? Would it tell her what had happened to Troy? Why her life had become a hell that she had no way of escaping?

Troy was not the same man she'd met in high school. He barely even resembled a man at all. He was a monster.

Something had happened to him, and she needed to know what. Why was he now so utterly evil? How could he do things that were impossible for a normal man? He was too strong and too fast. He heard things that it shouldn't be possible to hear and could see everything, regardless of how far away or how dark. It made escape impossible.

Sitting down on the chair as silently as she could, Evie scanned the screen. A file was open.

Project Arma. The words sat at the top of the document, clear as day.

What was Project Arma?

Skimming the information under the heading, she saw mentions of "drug trials" and "weapons".

Weapons for what? Skipping farther down, she came across a list. There were names. Lots of names.

Before she could read further, footsteps sounded outside the door.

Evie's heart went to her throat. How had he gotten to the door so quickly without her hearing?

There was no time to run or hide. Evie stood as the man of her nightmares entered the room. His eyes glimmered with malice as he took slow, threatening steps closer. It reminded her of how a lion might stalk its prey.

"Care to tell me what you're doing in my office, honey?" He spat the last word like it was acid on his tongue.

Swallowing hard, Evie tried to make her voice work. "I was just looking for a phone to call my parents." That was partially true. She did desperately want to speak to them. It wasn't the full truth, though—and Troy knew it.

"Why do you lie to me, Evaline?"

Evie glanced down, her eyes fixed on his fists, clenching and unclenching like an open threat. He took another step toward Evie. She felt cornered and helpless.

As her breaths came out shorter, her next step back was halted by the wall.

"I'm sorry," she whispered. What else could she say? She'd known what the consequences would be if she was caught, and she'd done it anyway.

Troy took another menacing step. She thought she might pass out from fear. She prayed that she would, knowing the cloak of darkness would protect her in the short term from whatever Troy had planned.

When he was a mere foot from Evie, his face contorted with fury. She was standing in front of a predator, waiting for him to end her.

Before she could blink, Troy swung his fist, hitting her in the jaw. Her head bashed against the wall before she crumpled to the floor.

The pain set her face on fire as blood trickled from her head. She opened her eyes just as Troy leaned down and grabbed her wrist. His fingers tightened until she heard the small bones snap.

Crying out, Evie tried to wrench her arms away, knowing it was a futile effort.

"You come in here again and I will break your legs so you can't stand for months, got it?"

Scrunching her eyes against the pain, Evie nodded.

"SAY IT!"

Opening her eyes, Evie was about to utter the words when she noticed the man who held her wrists in a death grip was no longer Troy. It was Luca.

Eyes popping open, Evie gasped in terror.

"Evie?"

At the feel of hands on her shoulders, Evie cried out and yanked herself free. Pushing herself back against the headboard, she wrapped her arms around her legs as fear threatened to choke her.

"Please leave me alone! Don't touch me. Please don't touch me!"

Ignoring the pain in her ribs and the ache in her face, she

cried as the terror of the nightmare washed over her. She made herself as small as possible.

Troy would never leave her, not in mind or body. The memory of him would always haunt her, and now it was jeopardizing what she might have with Luca.

After a few minutes, her breaths started to return to normal. As the nightmare receded, reality set in once again. She was in Luca's room. She was safe. For the moment.

Slowly raising her head, she mustered the courage to glance up. She saw Luca sitting next to her, a pained expression on his face. His hands remained at his side as he faced her, looking helpless.

A wave of guilt crashed over her at the knowledge that he looked that way because of *her*. This perfect man was trying so hard to help her, and she was doing nothing but hurting him.

Slowly, she moved onto her hands and knees and crawled into his lap, straddling him. When his arms didn't immediately wrap around her, Evie wrapped hers around his middle and hugged as tightly as she could. Eventually, she felt the warmth of Luca surround her as he gently pulled her closer. He was so careful, as if by moving too quickly, he'd scare her off.

Resting her face on his chest, Evie closed her eyes.

"I'm sorry. I didn't—"

"Don't apologize, sweetheart. Don't ever apologize for him. I want to help you so bad. I want to crawl into your head and protect you from your nightmares. But I can't protect you from the past, and that kills me."

Snuggling closer, Evie sighed. If she could, she would crawl into *his* body. It probably still wouldn't be close enough.

"Just you being here is the most healing I've experienced since I got away."

Luca's face nuzzled her hair. "I care about you, Evie."

She was a mess. She didn't know why this perfect man cared

about her, but she didn't want to question it. She'd spent enough time pushing him away.

"I care about you too, Luca. So much."

Slowing her breaths, Evie let the protection of Luca wash over her.

CHAPTER 19

*I*T HAD BEEN three days since Evie was attacked by that deadbeat. Three days and the team hadn't located him. It was like the guy was a damn ghost. Luca didn't understand how they hadn't found anything, even a scrap of evidence.

Walking into his kitchen, he watched Evie at the stove as she prepared dinner. Misty moved around her feet. The cat rarely left these days.

Evie had remained at his house, while he'd taken time off work. He wasn't returning until this shit was sorted. Luca wasn't taking any chances with her safety.

Moving to stand behind her, he wrapped his arms around her waist.

God, she felt good.

Nuzzling his face into her neck, he heard a giggle escape Evie's chest as she tried to squirm out of his hold. Pulling up his head, he kept his arms firmly around her waist. "Mmm, smells good, sweetheart, but you should be resting."

Turning her head, Evie tried pushing him back, but he didn't budge. "I can't stay in bed all day, Luca. I'll go crazy looking at the same four walls. And it may smell good, but don't be deceived, cooking is not my forte."

Lowering his lips again, Luca grazed her neck, sending a shiver down her spine. "I can think of lots of things you can do in that room other than looking at four walls."

Turning in his arms, she placed both hands on his chest. "Luca Kirwin. You can take your mind out of the gutter and leave me be. Dinner's just about ready, so make yourself useful and get us some cutlery."

Cracking a smile, Luca loosened his arms. "I love it when a woman tells me what to do."

Rewarded with a hint of a smile, Luca got to work setting the table. Making some space, he grabbed Evie's laptop to move it to the coffee table. She had only gone home to grab a few things, her laptop being one of them.

Every spare moment she had, she was on that thing. When Luca tried asking what she was working on, Evie was evasive and gave him noncommittal answers. The frustration of not knowing what she was doing was killing him, but he wanted to earn her trust. So, he let the subject drop. For now.

Scooping up two bowls of lasagna, Evie turned to place them on the table. Nibbling her bottom lip, she looked to be working up the courage to ask him something. Giving her the space she needed, Luca knew she would get there in her own time.

It wasn't until they were seated and had started eating that she finally voiced what she wanted to ask. "Have you found anything?"

She wanted to know about Troy.

It was obvious she was trying to hide her nerves, but the way she fidgeted with the wood on the edge of the table gave her away.

Luca hated that he couldn't tell her what she wanted to hear. Evie wanted to feel safe, and dammit, he wanted that too. "We're getting close."

Plastering a smile on her face, Evie nodded. Her gaze quickly turned back to her food. The disappointment behind the smile may have been invisible to most, but Luca could see it. Evie had been running from this asshole for the last year, and she needed him gone.

Indicating with his head to where the laptop sat, Luca asked the same question that he'd raised a few times in the last couple of days. "What were you working on today?"

The shuttered look came over her face. Disappointment sat heavily inside Luca. She was going to lie to him again.

"It's nothing, just looking up things to do in nearby towns."

Even though Luca had anticipated the lie, known it was coming, it still hurt. Telling himself not to read into it, Evie would share when she was ready, he reminded himself that he had secrets of his own he hadn't shared. Secrets he'd been debating telling her.

He *wanted* to share them with her. He wanted there to be no secrets in their relationship. He had even spoken to the team about telling Evie about the project and what it had done to him. The guys thought it was too soon. They asked him to wait.

The government had wanted it kept quiet. It definitely saved them from the attention and media frenzy, so the guys preferred it that way too.

They didn't share their past with people and kept their abilities to themselves.

But if he shared his secrets, she might share hers. If this thing was going to work, they needed to trust each other.

Clearing his voice, Luca glanced across the table at Evie. "Did Troy ever share anything with you about the work he was part of as a SEAL?"

Evie's eyes widened for a moment before she recovered. Shaking her head, she remained quiet.

He wanted to believe it was the truth, but could you really

date someone for that long and not know what they had been through? What they had become?

Deciding it was time to let Evie in, Luca stopped eating. "Do you remember that picture you found at Marble Protection?"

As she gave a small nod, Luca heard the pitter-patter of Evie's heart speeding up.

"We were sent on a rescue mission. It was supposed to be an easy in and out. We had the coordinates, knew the plan, should have been a three-day job. When we got there, we had a gut instinct that something wasn't right. Then we got an email from base to say the plans had changed and not to go ahead. None of it felt right, but as a SEAL, you don't go against orders. The next day, we heard the place we were supposed to raid blew up at the same time we were supposed to be in there. That afternoon, we ran into Troy and his team. They tried to make up some bullshit excuse as to why they were there, but we suspected the truth."

Visibly stiffening, Evie moved forward in her chair slightly. "You think Troy…"

When she was unable to finish the sentence, Luca did for her. "We think their directive had been to take us out. After the explosion, we were on the lookout for anything suspicious, so it would have been hard to take out our whole team."

Seeming to recover, Evie reached across the table and placed her hand on top of Luca's. "I'm glad you guys are all okay."

Turning his hand and wrapping his fingers around hers, Luca gave them a squeeze. "There's something else I want to tell you. The project that we were part of—"

Before Luca could finish what he was saying, a shadow moved past the kitchen window.

Rising to his feet, Luca pulled his phone from his back pocket and dialed Asher. He lived the closest and could get there fastest. At the same time, he took Evie's hand and pulled her to the corner of the room.

Asher answered on the first ring. "Hey, buddy."

"I need you to watch Evie," Luca said, not wasting any time.

"Be there in five."

Hanging up the phone, Luca glanced at the window again but saw nothing but the night sky. His body itched to go outside. Hunt the predator he knew was there. Luca wasn't making the same mistake Eden had made, though. He refused to leave Evie alone and unprotected.

Noticing the slight tremble in Evie's hand, Luca grimaced.

"What is it? What's going on?" Her voice was steady, but Luca could tell she was frightened.

Not wanting to alarm her, Luca pressed her farther into the corner. It was the only place in the house that would be invisible through the windows. "I might have seen something outside, but I'm not sure. I asked Asher to watch you for a moment while I check it out."

"Luca, no. If it's Troy, it's too dangerous. Please."

Rubbing her arms, Luca didn't move his gaze from Evie's. "Trust me, sweetheart. I'll be okay. I'm very well trained to deal with this sort of thing."

There was still fear in her eyes, but she nodded reluctantly.

When he was about to turn, Evie stopped him with her touch. "Be careful."

Moving his lips to her cheek, he placed a soft kiss there. "Always."

Three minutes later, Asher stepped inside Luca's front door. Walking over to a drawer, Luca discreetly tucked a gun into his waistband before passing Asher.

"Watch her like she's your own. Under no circumstances do you leave her unprotected. Got it?"

"Got it. Go, man."

Not waiting a moment longer, Luca moved to the back door and stepped outside.

The night air felt like a cold bucket of water on his face, but he barely felt it. He moved into the woods and through the trees.

To most, it would be pitch black, but to Luca, the trees and the dirt were crystal clear. He knew the darkness would have no advantage, because just as he could see everything, so could Troy.

Stopping for a moment, Luca closed his eyes and blocked out the sound of the wind and trees. He listened for anything that sounded human.

Then he heard it. It was the slightest of crackles. To his left was the sound of leaves crunching under footsteps.

Not stopping to think, Luca moved. He had one job. Catch the asshole and bury him.

The wind whipped across his face and branches broke beneath his feet. As he moved, the crackling of leaves became louder. Then he caught the sight of footprints in the dirt.

Pushing his body to move faster, Luca tracked the sounds. Troy may be fast, but Luca was faster.

Finally, he saw a figure.

Leaping forward, Luca hit the man in front of him at full speed. As the two powerful bodies collided, both grunted and dropped to the ground.

Pushing back to his feet, Luca got his first look at Troy in over a year. The son of a bitch hadn't changed.

The man's face pulled into a smile that made Luca's blood run cold.

"I hear you're shacking up with my woman, Rocket. I've never been much of a sharer, but for you, I'll make an exception."

Circling each other, neither man dropped their eyes.

"You'll never touch her again, and I'm going to tear you apart for what you've done to her."

Troy's brows lifted, but the smile remained. "No, you won't. I'm gonna get her back, and you won't be able to do shit about it. And when I do, what I've done previously will pale in comparison to what I have planned for her."

Luca's anger boiled over. All he saw was red. In the blink of an eye, he hooked Troy's neck with his elbow, holding him in a choke position.

All too quickly, Troy's elbow landed on Luca's ribs, effectively freeing him. Spinning, Troy pulled a fist back.

Dodging the hit, Luca bent and plowed into Troy's midsection. The hit took Troy by surprise, and he released a grunt. Not stopping, Luca slammed his knee into Troy's ribs, before punching his face.

The sounds of both men's hits were loud in the otherwise silent night.

Then Troy reached into his pocket.

Luca saw the glimmer of the blade just before it left Troy's fingers, the knife flying past his head.

Dodging the weapon gave Troy the time he needed to disappear.

Pulling out his gun, Luca moved fast, chasing the enemy, realizing the footsteps were taking him back toward the house. Back toward Evie.

Hell no.

Pushing his body faster than he ever had before, he followed the footprints. They led him to the window that looked directly into his living room.

No one had entered the house, but there were multiple prints on the ground. The asshole had been here before. Looking at the glass, Luca noticed Troy's handprint in mud on one side of the window. That was no accident. He'd left it there as a message.

Rage pulsed through Luca's veins. Had the fucker watched them together? He simultaneously wanted to be sick and murder the guy.

Turning to see where the footstep led, he tracked them to the street before they disappeared.

Only just keeping his frustration in check, Luca headed back inside. He would find Troy, and when he did, he would make him pay for every last bit of pain he'd put Evie through, plus more.

CHAPTER 20

*E*VIE WOKE TO the sound of voices in the living room.
Creeping out of bed, she moved silently across the room and sat next to the top of the stairs, ensuring she stayed out of sight. Hearing Luca's voice, she leaned closer.

"He was fucking messing with me. Going around in circles, making me chase him like a damn dog."

"So, you didn't get anything?" Bodie asked.

"Nothing. He's the same asshole he always was, but he's good. He wanted me to know that he's been here before. Wanted me to know that he can come and go as he pleases. Watch us whenever he wants, and there's not a damn thing I can do about it."

Evie flinched at the sound of a bang. It sounded like a boot connecting with a wall.

"What's the status on Cage and Ax?" Wyatt asked.

Asher's response was instant. "They'll be here at oh six hundred tomorrow."

"I want to find him. I have to find him *now*. What are we not seeing?" Luca's voice was angry.

Nibbling on her bottom lip, Evie tried to ignore the guilt she felt for bringing Troy back into Luca's life. If it wasn't for her, he wouldn't be feeling this way. He wouldn't be going through any of this.

"Something's not right." It was Mason, but he sounded a lot less agitated than Luca. "He could have taken or killed Evie at Marble Protection. He didn't. He left her. Then he said he was coming for you. Why?"

The reminder that she'd been so vulnerable made Evie shudder.

The men were quiet, then there was a shuffling creak, like someone sitting down on the couch. "Do you think he wants to take her again?"

Goose bumps rose along her arms at Asher's words.

"No. At least not right now. He would have taken her at Marble Protection if that was all he wanted." Wyatt's words lowered the anxiety inside Evie slightly. "There's something else he has planned."

"It has something to do with Project Arma." There was silence after Eden voiced his thoughts. Evie pressed closer to the stair railing, desperate to find out what they knew.

Please, please tell me what you know about the project. The idea of never finding out tore her apart.

"There *is* no Project Arma. Not anymore." Bodie sounded confident.

"Until we find everyone involved, we don't know that for sure," Luca said.

The next words were lost in their hushed voices.

Evie's heart dropped. No. She needed to know.

Feeling like she was choking on disappointment, Evie turned and tried to hold back the tears of frustration. Quietly returning to the bedroom, she spotted her laptop on the dresser. She went over and grabbed it before returning to the bed.

One way or another, she would find out. She would find out why Troy changed, why he'd killed her parents, and why he'd destroyed her life.

She couldn't have just chosen wrong, because that was too hard to accept. That meant it was all on her, right? If there was no third party, then the reason her parents were murdered was that she'd made a bad judgment call, and Evie just couldn't live with that.

Opening the laptop, she got to work. She wouldn't stop until she found the answers she was looking for.

What if the file *didn't* provide what she was looking for, though?

No. She wouldn't think about that.

Evie was madly typing when the bedroom door popped open. Quickly shutting the laptop, she glanced up. "Luca?"

Walking over to the bed, he began taking his clothes off, exhaustion on his face. As he removed his shirt, Evie's eyes were immediately drawn to his hard chest.

"What are you doing up? You should be sleeping," Luca said with his deep timbre.

Popping the laptop on the floor, Evie turned back to look at Luca. "I wasn't tired."

Drawing down the covers, he crawled into bed and pulled Evie close. "Mmm, you feel good."

Snuggling into his big body, she felt some of the tension in her own begin to ease. It was so easy with him. He made her feel like she was protected. Safe. Everything she had been chasing for the last year.

"What were you working on?"

Stiffening slightly, Evie's mind scrambled for a response. It wasn't that she was trying to hide it, exactly, but she wanted to get that damn file open before she told him. She didn't know why that was so important to her, beyond perhaps having more information before she exposed her last secret.

"It was nothing." Evie pushed down the guilt of having to lie. She knew he was hiding a part of himself from her, too, but for some reason, she couldn't let go of her own guilt.

"Tomorrow, I need to talk to you about something. Tonight, we sleep."

Hearing the disappointment in his voice, Evie's guilt intensified. "I would like that."

The muscles in Luca's arms rippled as he snuggled her closer. This man was everything. He had put her safety first tonight and was hunting the man of her nightmares to keep her safe.

Slowly leaning forward, Evie placed her lips on his. They were just as soft as she remembered, and, my lord, he smelled like heaven.

When Luca didn't pull away, Evie tried to deepen the kiss.

"Evie." Luca placed both hands on her shoulders. "I don't think this is a good idea right now."

Courage, Evie.

She wasn't going to take no for an answer. Not tonight.

Placing both her hands at the bottom of his shirt, she pushed it up to expose his rock-hard stomach. Brushing her finger over his muscles, she felt them harden and flex under her touch.

This man's body was like a sculpture. There wasn't an ounce of fat to be seen.

When Luca didn't move to stop her, she took advantage and leaned down to place soft kisses on his warm skin, slowly working her way up as her fingers trailed down the sides of his ribs.

A growl tore from Luca's throat as he gently took hold of her shoulders. Thinking Luca was going to push her away again, a relieved gasp escaped her lips when instead, he slowly pushed her back onto the mattress.

"We go slow, okay? You're still injured. If anything hurts, you tell me and we stop."

Nodding, Evie released a moan when Luca moved his lips to her cheek and trailed kisses down her throat. Letting out a cry of protest when he removed his mouth from her body, she settled again when he took hold of the end of her shirt and pulled it over her head. "You're addictive, Evie."

Then his lips were back on her neck.

Dropping her head, Evie felt his hand move to her breast and massage.

Arching her back, Evie reached down and cupped him. He was rock hard. Luca released another groan as he squeezed and tugged at her sensitive nipple.

Crying out, Evie writhed as a throbbing started deep inside her core. In tandem, his mouth lowered to her breast as his hand reached inside her underwear, using his thumb to massage her clit while his mouth suctioned her nipple. Evie squirmed beneath him, gasping when a small pain hit her ribs.

"Are you okay?" He started to move away, even as she nodded.

Unable to bear the thought of him ending his exploration, Evie reached inside his underwear and wrapped her fingers around him.

Stopping in his tracks, Luca hung his head and released a guttural growl.

Empowered by her effect on him, she began to move her hand up and down, feeling him swell in her grip, the muscles on his arms bunching.

"Evie…" His voice was hoarse.

"I need you, Luca."

Gripping the sides of her underwear, he quickly removed them. Moving his body down, he positioned his head above her center.

At the feel of his mouth on her clit, Evie buckled, almost exploding right there and then.

As the intensity of her pleasure hit, she tried to move her hips. Whether she was moving them away from or closer to Luca, she wasn't sure, but she was stopped by his firm hold, keeping her in place.

His tongue swiped across her clit. Evie's fingers latched onto the sheets around her. The pleasure was overpowering. As he focused on the sensitive spot, his mouth started to suction and pull.

Held too firm to do anything else, Evie thrashed her head. She felt drunk with lust. "Please, Luca, don't make me wait." She gasped the words, wanting him inside her.

Finally releasing her, Luca reached into the bedside table before covering himself with a condom. Moving his body back over hers, resting all his weight on his hands, he spread her thighs with his hips.

Placing himself at her entrance, he slowly slid inside her.

She shut her eyes at the intense sensation of him filling her so completely.

Once they were fused together, Luca stopped, waiting for her muscles to relax. Veins bulging at his evident self-restraint, he held still above her.

Not wanting to wait any longer, Evie raised her head and nibbled on his lip. Pushing her tongue into his mouth, she silently pleaded for him to move.

Luca lifted his hips, easing back before lowering again. His pace was agonizingly slow. Trying to move her hips to meet his, she was stopped by Luca's hands on her waist, holding her tightly.

She released a whimper when he moved a hand down to massage her clit. She felt like she was dying a slow death as the heat built in her core so agonizingly slowly.

Dropping his head to Evie's neck, Luca bit the sensitive spot beneath her ear. His ravaging mouth, in combination with his gentle thrusts, was tormenting.

He quickened his pace slightly but continued to hold her in place, no doubt conscious of her cracked ribs.

Evie's tenacious fingers latched onto his skin.

Just when she thought she couldn't take it anymore, her body shattered. She cried out as Luca kept thrusting, prolonging the orgasm. Shutting her eyes, she heard his groan just as he stiffened and shuddered through his own climax.

Both breathing heavily, there was a moment of silence between them before Luca's eyes raised to hers. Still connected, something passed between them. No words were needed, but the emotions were strong.

Placing a gentle kiss on her lips, Luca moved to lie beside her, pulling her close.

Coming down from the high, she felt something settle inside of her. Peace. This great protector beside Evie cared about her, and she cared about him. Luca had seen her, even when all she had done was try to run and hide from him.

It was like a weight had been lifted from her chest, and she could breathe again.

Closing her eyes, Evie began to drift to sleep, Luca's arms like a shield against everything wrong in the world. Maybe things would work out. Maybe she would be okay after all. "Thank you." She whispered the words.

"For what?"

"Everything."

Arms tightening around her, Luca pulled her closer. "No, thank you, sweetheart, for letting me in."

Snuggling closer to Luca, she prayed that he could be her happy ending.

CHAPTER 21

*A*S LIGHT FILTERED into the bedroom, Evie reached across the bed for Luca. When her hand felt nothing but cool sheets, her eyes popped open and she shot up.

Grimacing, her hand went to her ribs. Even though it had been a few days since the attack, she knew the pain of fractured ribs would linger for a while.

Slowly climbing out of bed, Evie wrapped her robe around her shoulders, grabbing the laptop before heading downstairs.

Stepping into the living room, she stopped in her tracks.

There was a very large, muscular man in the room, but it wasn't Luca. Or anyone she recognized. He looked to be as big as Eden, both in height and breadth. The man turned. He was gorgeous, with his almost-black eyes and midnight hair.

Realizing she was staring, Evie flicked her gaze back to his face. She should probably be scared, but being in Luca's house, she felt safe, knowing he was likely nearby if there was trouble.

"I was wondering when the alluring Evie Scott would rise and shine."

Raising her brows, Evie found herself at a loss for words.

Then she heard the back door open and shut before Asher walked in.

"Yo, bro, Luca needs to sort out that garden situation, a whole SWAT team could hide in those bushes and never be seen." Turning toward Evie, Asher cracked a smile. "You're up! Finally. We were considering breaking Luca's 'no one goes in the bedroom' rule."

Smoothing her hair, Evie finally remembered that she hadn't actually looked at herself in the mirror yet. God, she must be a mess. Feeling self-conscious, she pulled her robe a bit tighter.

"Darlin', you look fine." The stranger gave Evie a wink before dropping his gigantic form onto Luca's couch.

Asher walked up to the man and hit him on the back of the head. "Don't be rude. Introduce yourself to Evie."

The man gave her another confident smile. "I'm Kye, but the guys call me Cage. I'm also the best looking of the bunch, as you've probably noticed."

At the intensity of his gaze, she felt her cheeks heat up.

Just then, the front door opened, and Luca and Wyatt walked in. Spotting Evie immediately, Luca headed straight for her, wrapping his arm around her waist. "Morning, sweetheart. Wyatt and I just went for a run," he said. Nodding his head, he indicated to where Kye was sitting. "Did you meet Cage?"

"Oh, we met, Rocket." Kye gave Evie another wink.

Luca let out a growl. "Get your damn eyes off my woman."

Putting up his hands, Kye cast his gaze to the side window. "Whatever you say, man."

Evie put her hand on Luca's chest. "I'm going to go get changed."

Rubbing his hand up her arm, he nodded. "Okay."

As she turned to go, Wyatt's voice stopped her. "Can I borrow the laptop? This guy doesn't have a decent piece of technology, and I just want to check something."

Looking down, Evie had forgotten she was holding the thing. "Oh, sure."

Handing it over, Evie headed back upstairs, straight to the bathroom to shower. Once she was standing under the stream of water, she closed her eyes and let the warmth soothe her sore body.

About ten minutes in, the glass door cracked open and Luca stepped inside.

Too surprised to say anything, she stood still as Luca's arms wrapped around her waist. His powerful body took up almost all the space in the shower stall. Lowering his head, he began to nuzzle the side of her neck.

"Luca, the guys are right out there."

As his mouth trailed down Evie's shoulder, a small shiver ran up her spine. "Negative, I sent those assholes home." Luca lifted her arms and placed them on his shoulders. Then, reaching down, he grabbed her legs and pulled them around his waist. As he held her bare body against his, Evie lay her head against his shoulder.

At some point, the embrace changed from being sexual to something else entirely.

Evie wasn't sure how long they stood under the stream of water, but the position was so intimate. Skin against skin. This was the closest she'd ever felt to another human.

Too soon, the water started to chill. Reaching over, Luca turned it off.

"How are your ribs, sweetheart?" he asked, breaking the silence.

"They're okay."

A growl rumbled from his chest as he stepped outside the shower with Evie still in his arms. "I hate that you're in pain."

Pulling a large towel from the rack, Luca wrapped it around both of them. Once in the bedroom, he placed Evie on the bed, giving her a kiss before moving away. "What should we do today?"

Evie knew what she *wanted* to do. Seeing Luca wearing nothing, water droplets dripping from his naked chest, had her feeling flushed. But she knew she needed to heal. She would settle for watching, for now, even if it was pure torture. "I'm fine with another day at home. I need to work on my laptop a bit anyway."

Motionless for a moment before continuing to open his drawer, Luca questioned, "What do you need to work on?" Turning, he watched her closely.

"I've just been working on something. Once it's done, I want to share it with you."

Well, it wasn't the full confession he was probably hoping for, but at least she hadn't totally made something up like the previous times he'd asked.

Luca pulled on his clothes before walking back to Evie, bending down, so only a couple of inches separated their faces. "I would love for you to share, sweetheart."

As he kissed her forehead, Evie prayed that she could hack the file soon, so that no more secrets separated them.

It was midafternoon when the sound of ringing pulled Luca away from his workout. Dropping the weight to the floor of his workout room, he reached for his phone.

"Striker, what's happening?"

"Team meeting in ten. I'm a couple minutes from your place. I'll stay with Evie and be part of the meeting over the phone."

Frowning, Luca was already pulling a shirt over his head. "What's the meeting for, and why's it so important *I'm* there when you're not?"

"Not sure, man, just doing what Jobs asked."

Already hearing Asher's car pull up out the front, Luca hung up the phone and headed into the bedroom. Evie was sitting on the bed working on her laptop. When her green eyes met his, Luca almost forgot what he'd entered the room to say. It would be so easy to say "screw it all" and just stay and get lost in her.

Reluctantly, Luca walked over to the bed. "There's a meeting at Marble. Asher's on the couch. Be back soon, okay?"

"Okay." Evie smiled as Luca bent to kiss her. He stayed a moment or two longer than he'd intended.

"You're too damn enticing, you know that?" His words were spoken against her lips.

Eyes twinkling, Evie turned back to her laptop. "If that were true, you would be under the covers with me right now, ditching this meeting of yours."

With a growl, Luca exited the room. Damn, he wished he could do exactly that.

When he reached for his keys, he glanced at Asher lying back on his couch, eating chips. "Watch the crumbs, asshole."

"Come on, Rocket, I know how much you love cleaning. Consider my sloppiness a favor."

Rolling his eyes, Luca headed for the door. "Whatever. Be back soon."

"I'll be listening!"

As Luca made his way to the car, he wondered again what this was all about. Why would the team be meeting after just speaking last night?

They still didn't know what Troy wanted. It was more than just Evie, of course. Otherwise, he would have taken her when he had the chance.

The team was also sure of one other thing: Troy knew more about Project Arma than they did. That meant whoever caught him first, the objective wasn't to kill him, but to get information.

The trip was quick. As soon as Luca stepped into the office, he knew he wasn't going to like whatever was said.

Wyatt sat at the end of the table, laptop open in front of him.

Mason and Bodie were next to him, looking more disappointed than anything. Eden leaned against the wall looking positively murderous.

"What is it?"

Wyatt looked up. "You should sit, Rocket. We wanted to tell you this in person."

Stopping at the end of the table, Luca crossed his arms. "No. Tell me what's going on."

Wyatt held his gaze. "It's Evie."

Pausing, Luca tried to hide the shot of anxiety. "What? Did Troy show up again? Did you find out what he wants?"

Mason ran his hand through his hair. "Jobs found something on her computer."

What the hell? "When? This morning? You snooped through her shit?"

Raising both his hands, Wyatt pushed back from the table. "Rocket, I wasn't looking. It was already open when I used the laptop."

Knowing he didn't want the answer to the question, he asked anyway. "What was?"

"The Project Arma file we've been trying to crack. She's also working on it."

Luca's world fractured slightly. No. That wasn't possible. "She can't hack files."

"Well, she's trying." Mason's voice was solemn.

"Are you sure?"

"Yes," Wyatt said, looking disappointed.

Knowing there was no way Wyatt would call the meeting unless he was one hundred percent sure, the truth cut into Luca. He knew she loved working on computers, but how did she get the file in the first place?

Turning, Luca ran his hands through his hair before facing his team again. "Okay, so what does this mean? That she knows about the project we were part of?"

Eden broke his silence. "It means that she knows a lot more than she's let on. She knows how to hack. She probably knows about the project. She also knows what we're capable of."

She'd alluded to Troy's abilities a few times, so that part wasn't a huge surprise.

Wyatt cleared his voice. "There's more." Luca swallowed as his dread intensified. "I found her real identity."

Wyatt pushed the laptop across the table toward Luca. He stared at the damn piece of technology for a moment like it was a bomb about to go off, before pulling it in front of himself.

A file sat open, about an Evaline Scali.

Evaline.

Taking a breath, Luca started to read the information. Graduated top of her class and offered scholarships to study Information Technology at a dozen colleges across the country. Went to a college close to home but dropped out a couple of years in.

Why hadn't she told him any of this? Did she not trust him with it?

Wyatt's voice drew Luca's eyes off the screen. "She tried to erase that information. That alone would have taken extremely advanced knowledge. I had to dig deep, and I mean *deep*, to find it. She created the new profile of herself as Evie Scott. Looks damn real too."

Mason stood and put his hands in his pockets. "We knew she was hiding something. That something is now connected to *us*. We need answers, Rocket."

He was right. Luca was still confident she wasn't one of the bad guys, but he needed to know where she'd gotten the file and why she was hacking it. He needed to think of the safety of his team. His brothers. "I'll get them."

Eden's gaze swung to Luca. "I don't think she's a threat, but we need the truth."

They needed the truth as much as Luca did.

CHAPTER 22

SHUTTING DOWN HER laptop, Evie stretched her sore muscles. Sitting in the same spot all day was not good for her recovering body.

Glancing at the time, she noticed it was already late afternoon. Shifting off the bed, she headed into the kitchen. Passing Asher on the way, she noticed he had an earpiece in and seemed to be listening intently.

"Staying for dinner, Asher?"

Without looking up, he shook his head. "Nah, Rocket will be back soon."

Hesitating for a moment before continuing to the kitchen, Evie frowned. There was something about Asher's response that gave her pause. Typically, he would joke around, tease her...then head into the kitchen and eat all the food.

Taking out the earpiece, Asher started fiddling with his phone. Evie waited a moment to see if he might say anything else, but when he remained silent, she continued to the kitchen.

Mentally shrugging off his unusual behavior, Evie opened the back door and let Misty in. Giving her a quick pat, she fed Misty before making a start on dinner.

She was making an easy roast chicken tonight. Evie wouldn't describe herself as a good cook at all, but she knew Luca appreciated her efforts. Glancing back toward Asher, she wondered again what might be going on with him. Maybe he was fighting with Lexie?

Now that Evie knew the secret Luca had been keeping from her, she'd bet it was the same secret Asher kept from Lexie.

Starting to peel potatoes, Evie glanced up at the sound of the door opening. As Luca stepped inside, she couldn't stop the sudden rush of giddy excitement she always felt when she saw him.

Evie tried to tamper the disappointment when he gave Asher a nod before heading upstairs.

Strange. He didn't even acknowledge her. Evie tried not to let it bother her.

Turning her attention back to the job at hand, she thought about the evening ahead of them. She'd already decided it was time to share a bit more about herself and her past with Luca. Sharing her remaining secrets scared her, but the fear of losing Luca was greater. It was like ripping off the last part of the mask that had protected her for a year, but there was no alternative. They couldn't last with secrets between them, she knew that.

Evie just hoped that he understood why she hadn't told him everything earlier.

Turning from the sink with potatoes in hand, Evie let out a screech at seeing Luca standing right behind her. Just saving herself from dropping the potatoes, she placed a hand to her chest.

"Luca! You scared me. Make a noise or something when you move."

"Sorry, sweetheart." Luca placed a kiss on her cheek, smiling before turning away. A smile that didn't quite reach his eyes.

An uneasy feeling started to creep in. Something was off.

First, Asher was acting strange, and now Luca. It wasn't in her head.

Before Luca could walk away, Evie placed a hand on his arm. When he turned, she studied his face for a moment, searching for anything that would give her a clue to what was going on. "Is everything okay?" she asked, trying to keep the nervousness out of her voice.

There was a slight pause before Luca spoke. "Of course. I'll set the table."

The next half-hour passed in complete silence. She gave several nervous glances Luca's way, but words eluded her.

Don't overthink this, Evie.

She was being dumb. The whole Troy situation was probably just playing on his mind.

Finished with dinner, she placed both plates of food on the table before sitting opposite Luca. Glancing up, Evie noticed that his eyes were on her. Squirming beneath his intense gaze, she diverted her attention back to her food.

Clearing her voice, Evie gathered the courage to ask the question that had been playing on her mind. "How did the meeting go?"

Luca swallowed a bite of chicken. "Wyatt discovered some interesting information about the case we've been working on. It was a bit surprising."

Nodding, Evie nibbled on her bottom lip, losing her appetite. "It must have been important information. You seem a bit off."

Shrugging, Luca popped some more food into his mouth before answering. "It's one of those things where you knew there was missing information, but what you found wasn't quite what you expected."

Okay, that would explain the bad mood. "Do you know what you'll do with the information?"

Placing his fork down, Luca nodded. "I'm going to try to dig deeper. Find out the exact details."

Almost too scared to ask, Evie put her own fork down. "Why just you? What about the rest of the team?"

Luca's gaze was intense. Most of the time, Evie forgot just how deadly he was, but at this moment, he looked every bit of it. "I'm the closest to it."

The bad feeling in Evie's gut intensified, her hands becoming clammy. Was he talking about her? Had they discovered something she wasn't telling them? If that was the case, why didn't he just ask? Why all this wordplay?

Luca's voice broke into Evie's thoughts. "What did you get into while I was gone?"

Pushing her almost-full plate aside, Evie gave up trying to eat the food. Choosing her words carefully, she looked Luca straight in the eye. "Not much. Used my laptop a bit, made dinner."

Something Evie couldn't describe flashed through Luca's eyes. Taking another bite, Luca finally broke the eye contact. "I want there to be no secrets between us, Evie."

Swallowing, she nodded. "Me too, Luca."

"There are things I need to tell you. Things I haven't shared that I have to, if this thing between us is going to work." *If* it was going to work? "I've wanted to tell you, but I wanted to build on our relationship a bit first. I'm confident in us, Evie...but I'm going to ask you something that I have no right to ask. I'd like to know *your* secrets, before I share mine."

Sweat beaded on her forehead. He knew. Whether he knew about the file or that she'd lied about her name, she wasn't sure, but he knew something, and he was giving her a chance to tell him willingly.

She wanted to tell him. She had planned to, but now that the time had come, it suddenly felt impossible. She would be naked. She would be placing all her trust in another soul. Did Luca really understand how hard that was for her?

Suddenly standing, Evie couldn't remain where she was.

Luca rose from his chair too. He was so large that he towered over her. She'd never felt intimidated by his size, but right then, she did.

"I have secrets, Luca, but trust doesn't come easily for me." Trying to keep the tears at bay, Evie couldn't let herself fall apart. There was nothing she wanted more than to share the final parts of herself with him. But there was something blocking her. Something deep down screaming at her that if she let someone else in completely, she was leaving herself open to the past repeating itself.

"I understand. But there are things I need to know—and I need to know them *now*." Luca's voice softened slightly. She saw part of the old Luca rather than the interrogator who had returned this afternoon. "Trust me, Evie."

As she searched his eyes for an answer, her nerves almost swallowed her. When she took a small step back, Luca remained where he was, but his eyes tracked her movement.

"I have no bad intentions toward you or the team."

Luca cocked his head. "Then it doesn't matter if I know who you really are."

Evie's heart stopped. "Who I really am?"

Luca remained silent, watching her intently.

He knew who she really was. Did that mean he knew her name? The only person who had spoken it in recent years was Troy. She associated that name with so much pain and ugliness. She couldn't bear to hear it spoken by Luca.

"Wyatt found my real name." Of course he did. From what Luca had told her, he could find anything, no matter how deeply it was hidden.

Giving the slightest nod, Luca's voice came out in a whisper as he said the name Evie tried to forget. "Evaline?"

At the sound of her full name, Evie's heartbeat tripled. It sounded wrong coming from him, like he shouldn't speak it after she'd heard it so many times from Troy.

"Don't call me that! No one's called me that since—" She

couldn't finish the sentence.

"Since Troy."

"It's a constant reminder of who I was then. Of the life I lived." Evie took another step back. "He locked me in the house for years. Do you know that? I couldn't get out. He would get into these moods where he just wanted to pick a fight, which led to abuse, and I couldn't escape. I was trapped. A prisoner! Do you know what that's like? Hearing that name brings back *everything*. I can't say it or hear it without feeling the pain of the past."

"It's okay, Evie."

"I'm not *her*, Luca. I haven't been her since I got away. That's why I didn't tell you. I can't even think about her." The tears trickled down her cheeks. "She was broken. She missed all the signs."

Evie remained silent as Luca took a step forward. She took another big step back. She felt stalked. Crowded. There was no space in this damn room.

"Do you know what he's capable of?" Luca asked, though Evie knew he already had the answer.

Of course she knew. It starred in her nightmares. His impossible strength, his speed. Troy's ability to hear her every movement. It made the idea of escape almost hopeless.

Evie's voice was quiet. So quiet she barely heard herself speak. "Yes."

Luca's expression didn't change. "Do you know about the project he was part of?"

Shaking her head, Evie held her ground. "Only that it was called Project Arma. That soldiers who were part of the project have enhanced...abilities."

Luca nodded, remaining still. Then he indicated with his head upstairs. "What have you been doing on your laptop, Evie?"

So, he knew about that too. Had Wyatt uncovered everything about her, down to the last minute detail? "I'm trying to open a file."

Thinking he'd ask what the file was, his next question came as a surprise. "How do you know how to open it?"

Crossing her arms, Evie shrugged. "I'm good at hacking."

At the absence of any surprise on his face, Evie realized Wyatt must have found her college history too. "Where'd you get the file from?"

Thinking back to that day sent a shiver down Evie's spine. "I stole it from Troy. Before I ran."

Luca seemed closer...but she hadn't seen him move. "Why?"

This was the question. The one she didn't want to answer, because that really would leave her soul bare. Evie shrugged. "Because I wanted to."

"That's a lie, Evie. Tell me why you're hacking that file."

Turning around, Evie took several steps away from him— only to find him standing right in front of her. The speed that Luca had just displayed was like nothing she'd ever seen. Even from Troy. It seemed impossible that he'd gotten around her so fast.

Wasn't that what this was all about though? That he and others like him were capable of the impossible?

Her eyes darted around the room as she took another step back.

"I'm not going to hurt you, Evie. I just need to know."

A tear dropped down Evie's cheek. "Why do you need to know?"

About to move another step away, she was thwarted when Luca's hand shot out and grabbed onto hers. His fingers were gentle but firm. "Please, sweetheart. This is just you and me. You know you're safe with me. I need the truth."

Evie's voice rose. "I took it because I need to *know*, Luca. I need to know it's not my fault!"

Luca cocked his head while his thumb stroked her wrist. "What's not your fault?"

Choking on her tears, Evie almost laughed. *"Everything.* You want to know my biggest secret? The one I try to keep from everyone? I'm completely broken! Shattered. Some days I feel like I can't even breathe. It takes all my strength to just get out of bed. Since meeting you, I feel better, but I'm still not whole. And it's because of *him*. *He* did this. I was okay before. I *hate* him!"

Knowing she sounded hysterical, Evie couldn't stop. She began shouting. "I let myself become a victim to a monster, and because of that, I got my parents killed."

Her heart broke at the words coming out of her mouth. "I risked my life to steal that file because I have to know that it's not completely my fault, because if it is, I can't live with myself. I need confirmation that my parents aren't dead because I was too stupid, too blind. I took extra time that I didn't have to go into his office and take a USB from his desk before I ran. I've been madly trying to find a reason that doesn't end with *everything* being my fault, and I am placing all my hopes on that file."

There it was. Evie's secrets were all out in the open. Her legs gave out as sobs tore through her chest.

Luca caught her easily in his arms and pulled her off her feet. Cradling Evie, he walked to the couch. Sitting on his lap, she let the sobs consume her.

"I did it, Luca. I killed my parents! They were trying to help me escape, and he broke into their house and murdered them because of *me*."

Placing his lips near her ear, Luca's voice was gentle. "Shhh, it's okay, sweetheart."

Unable to control the heartache that tore through her chest, Evie shook her head. "No. It hasn't been okay for a long time, Luca."

CHAPTER 23

$\mathcal{T}$HE SOBS RACKED Evie's body. Luca wished he could take away her pain. Erase it from her past. He wanted to go back and save her from the monster that was Troy.

He settled for holding her and making a promise to himself that nothing like that would ever happen to her again.

Remorse ate at him. He regretted how he'd approached this tonight, but the moment he heard she was trying to hack the Project Arma file, it was like history repeating itself. He'd trusted the wrong people before. Placed his trust in a system that saw him as a tool to use as they wished. Others on his team struggled with trust far more than him, but Luca still found it hard to completely let go.

Never again. He would trust Evie. She was his to trust and protect now.

Noticing she had gone quiet, Luca looked down to see her staring at a blank spot on the wall. "How did you get away, sweetheart?"

Her voice was small. "He slipped one day. He never slipped. Maybe he thought he'd finally broken me, that I wouldn't try to leave. When I left my room, I saw the keys. At first, I thought I was seeing things. Hallucinating maybe, seeing what I wanted to see. When my mind finally realized the keys were real, the fear inside of me was like nothing I'd ever experienced. I had to make a snap decision whether to attempt an escape and live with the consequences if I got caught, or stay in the hell he'd built for me and continue trying to survive. I decided to leave.

"I grabbed a small bag and packed just a few essentials. Then used the keys to open the office door. I took the USB from the laptop, not even knowing if it had any information I could use… then just ran. He must have been quite a distance from the house, because even though he came after me, he never caught me. He was fast, Luca. So much faster than me."

Glancing down at her hands, Luca saw a slight tremble in them. He engulfed her hands in one of his own.

"I ran through the woods, straight onto the highway. A truck hit me, and the next thing I knew, I woke up in a hospital bed. The driver had rushed me there. He must have slowed down quite a lot because I got away with only a concussion and a ton of scrapes and bruises. I knew it wouldn't be long until Troy located me, so I grabbed my stuff and ran minutes after waking. It wasn't hard. I'd learned how to push past injuries long before."

"You're a damn strong woman, Evie. How did you survive with basically just the clothes on your back?"

Evie shrugged. "I sold some of the things that I took. Stayed hidden for the first couple weeks. I used public computers to create my background, never the same one twice. When I was confident enough, I moved to another town and worked for a short while. It was hard, but at the same time, it felt like I'd gained a small part of myself back. A small chunk of freedom."

Luca ground his teeth. She was running and hiding, and she considered that freedom? Troy didn't deserve mercy, and Luca sure as hell wouldn't be granting him any when he found the asshole.

Stroking Evie's arm again, he felt humbled that she'd shared her history with him. She'd trusted him. It was time to trust her.

"We didn't know."

Evie glanced up at Luca, confused.

"My team. We didn't know what Project Arma really was. Until after."

Evie looked surprised but remained silent.

"We were SEALs. We did what we were told. So, when we got notice that we were required to participate in a covert project, that's what we did." Wiping a tear from her cheek, Luca continued. "The purpose of the project was to show improved recovery time through a series of injections and by participating in training and fitness programs tailored to our specific needs. Make us more efficient. We didn't question it. Why would we? We just trusted the system and thought we were working for the good guys."

"But you weren't?"

Luca met Evie's gaze, thinking back to all the signs his team had missed. "Those running the project were offered money from people in high places to go rogue. The scientists, medical staff, even our commander were all on someone's payroll, happy to sacrifice the lives of others so they could earn some extra money. We were the guinea pigs. These people created a drug that could turn normal SEALs and soldiers into weapons. Make an army that would be unstoppable. We're not sure exactly what the end goal was. We're still working on it."

Evie's frown got deeper. "I'm really sorry, Luca."

He glanced out the window. "We were actually the lucky ones. There were unknowing participants in the project who received earlier versions of the drug. Most didn't survive."

The familiar anger returned at what those men must have gone through. The feel of Evie's hand on his chest soothed some of the turmoil. "That's terrible."

"We were one of the last teams recruited. The drug was more established by then. Tried and tested."

"This probably makes me really selfish, but I'm glad you were part of it when they had a better version of the drug." Evie looked down at his chest. "Do you think they made a drug that could change a man's mental state? They must have had a plan to make their subjects compliant. Maybe that's what they did to Troy?"

The desperation in Evie's voice was clear. She needed the validation that this wasn't her fault. "I want to be honest, sweetheart. I don't know. We all wonder every day how they planned to make us work for them after the drugs took effect. It's possible they came up with another drug to make soldiers more malleable. No matter what, we're going to find out."

The disappointment shone in Evie's green eyes, although she tried to mask it. "Okay," she said, smoothing the wrinkles on Luca's shirt. His skin warmed at her touch. "So, no one found anything when they closed down the project and arrested everyone?"

The memory of how it ended caused fresh anger to pulse through Luca's veins. "No. The government found out about the project from an anonymous source. Unfortunately, we think someone also told the people working there, because just before the raid, most people on the payroll disappeared. They took almost all the evidence with them. The team is quietly working with the government to find every last person who was involved. They're out there, we just need to locate them."

"How…how did you get the file?"

"Someone sent it to us. We're not sure who. For all we know, it could be the same person who tipped off the government about the project. They included a note that said it was taken from Project Arma while the program was still running."

"Wow." Evie's brows rose. "Wyatt and I could work together on cracking the file. I'm so close, Luca, and with another head to help, it will be even faster."

How could he have ever questioned this woman's loyalty? "That sounds like a good idea, sweetheart."

There was another pause, where Luca could tell Evie was working up the courage to say something else. "When, um, when you met Troy. Was he a...good person, do you think?"

Evie was searching Luca's eyes, craving a certain answer. Again, he wished he could give her what she needed. "I only met him a couple of years ago. He wasn't a nice person then, sweetheart. That's not to say he was always like that, though. His team was recruited before mine. Probably given an earlier version of the drug."

Evie nodded and nibbled on her lip. "How...how do you know he wasn't good?"

There had never been any question in Luca's mind that Troy wasn't a good person. "Part of it was the feeling I got when I looked into his eyes. He lacked a level of compassion that most people have. He used to get a thrill out of killing. Would come back after a mission and almost brag about it. A soldier should only kill out of necessity, and never do we feel proud after. There were other things, too, like when we were training. He would always try to take things too far. Wouldn't care if he injured fellow soldiers."

Nodding, Evie looked down at her hands. "Thank you for sharing with me, and I'm sorry I didn't tell you the truth sooner."

"Evie, I withheld facts from you too. We're both at fault. Now you know you can tell me anything, right? I judge a person by what's in here," Luca placed his hand over her heart, "not what is or isn't on paper."

Giving him a small smile, Evie rested her head on his chest as she shut her eyes. "I like you, Luca. A lot."

Placing a kiss on her head, he tightened his arms around her. "I like you too, Evie. A bit more than a lot, I think." At her yawn, Luca stood, keeping her firmly against his chest. "It's still early, but I think it's time to get you to bed."

"Hmm." Evie's chest was already rising and falling at a steady rhythm.

Once he reached the bedroom, Luca placed her on the mattress, making quick work of removing her top and pants before dragging the sheet from beneath her and covering her body.

Evie's eyes fluttered open for a moment.

"I'll be right back, darlin', just going to lock up," he said.

Knitting her brows together, Evie placed her hand on his arm. "I'm glad we have no secrets anymore."

Covering her hand with his own, Luca smiled. "Me too, sweetheart."

Closing her eyes, Evie rolled onto her side. "I trust you, Luca."

Good, because a relationship without trust was never going to go anywhere.

Walking out of the room, Luca shut the door before pulling out his phone and dialing Asher.

He answered on the first ring. "How'd it go?"

Luca waited until he was downstairs to speak. "She took the file when she ran from him, and she took it because she wanted to find out what had happened to Troy. Why he'd changed. She's not a threat to us. She's innocent, and she needs our help."

"You trust her?"

"Yes." There was no pause and no hesitation for Luca.

"Then I trust her too, and so will the team. I'll pass on the information. You look after your woman."

"Striker…"

"Yeah, buddy?"

Luca's voice grew dark. "When we find him, I get to kill that fucker. Got it?"

"We need to get answers from him, Rocket," Asher said cautiously.

Yes. But if they didn't get what they wanted, or even if they did, Luca would still end him. "And I need him dead."

Asher sighed, probably realizing fighting Luca on this was pointless. "Got it."

CHAPTER 24

"WHY, GOOD MORNING, Mr. and Mrs. Love Birds."

As Evie entered Marble Protection, hand clasped in Luca's, Lexie gave them a massive grin from behind the front counter.

Lexie crossed her arms. "So, we official yet? Can you finally admit to the world that you're obsessed with each other?"

"Sure can, Lexie."

Glancing at Luca's words in surprise, Evie blushed.

"Finally! I've been waiting weeks for this. You better treat my girl right though, Luca, or you'll have me to answer to."

His hand tightened slightly around Evie's. "Plan on it."

Moving around the desk, Lexie wrapped Evie in her arms, mindful of her injuries. "You deserve to be happy, Evie," she whispered. Pulling back, she turned to Luca and gave him a punch on the arm. "Remember—*me* to deal with."

Evie had to stop herself from laughing when Lexie pointed to her eyes, then to Luca. He was easily double the woman's size, but Evie was sure that wouldn't stop Lexie.

God, she was lucky to have someone like Lex in her life.

Pulling Evie down the hall, Luca dragged her into the office. Wyatt glanced up from behind the table.

"Ready to get to work?" Wyatt's words were succinct as he looked up briefly, only to go straight back to focusing on the screen in front of him.

The sight of him brought on some nervous flutters. The trust wasn't quite there. She could see it in his eyes. Standing straighter, Evie pulled out her laptop and moved across the room to sit down next to him. Well, then, it was her job to convince him otherwise wasn't it?

"Ready." Evie opened her laptop, getting straight to the job at hand. She felt Luca's kiss on her temple but didn't look up. She was going to crack the file today if it killed her, but she had to focus.

Wyatt and Evie worked in silence for over an hour. Every so often, they would glance at each other's screen, but they may as well have been in different rooms.

She studied Wyatt for a moment from the corner of her eye. He may have a hacker's brain, but he was built like a SEAL. Similar to all the other guys, Wyatt's shirt was pulled tightly over his torso, showing off his incredible size and strength. He wouldn't fool anyone in an actual office.

Eventually, frustration started to build at both their lack of progress and the deafening silence. Removing her fingers from the keyboard, Evie turned to face Wyatt. "I'm not the bad guy, you know."

Wyatt kept his eyes straight ahead. "So Luca's told me."

"You don't believe him?"

Stopping what he was doing, Wyatt angled his body toward Evie. Just like when any of the others were close, Evie felt dwarfed by his size. The mere breadth of his shoulders was double, maybe even triple, hers.

"I want to believe you, Evie, and I'm trying. The problem is, I've seen people swear up and down that their intentions were one thing, only to find out otherwise."

Some of Evie's anger faded. "I can understand that. I'm sorry about what happened."

Searching Evie's eyes, Wyatt frowned. "You want to know what Luca is? What I am? What we all are? We're weapons. And before that, we were unknowing test subjects. Those men and I have been through hell together. We protect each other. But none of us foresaw what eventually happened to us—and we all feel guilty for letting each other down. We don't want that to happen again. So, trust doesn't come easy. For any of us."

"I get it. And trust doesn't come easy for me either. But I'm a damn good hacker, and I want to open this file as much as you do." Taking a breath before she continued, Evie softened her voice. "Also, you and your brothers are more than weapons. They may have tried to turn you into one, but what you're capable of doesn't define who you are."

"One thing we *know* we are is brothers."

Nodding, a slight smile lit her face. "And I think that's great."

Sitting back, Wyatt crossed his arms over his gigantic chest. "So…this thing between you and Luca is real?"

Evie nodded. "It's real to me." As he watched her for a moment, Evie tried not to squirm under his scrutiny.

"Welcome to the family then." Turning back to his computer, Wyatt started typing again as if nothing had happened.

Evie's brows rose. That was it? Did he go from not trusting her to trusting her after one conversation?

"Back to work, Scott. We've got a file to open."

Feeling a little lighter, Evie turned back to her computer.

From that point on, they worked as a team. Sharing information and helping each other when needed. By midafternoon, Evie's eyes were beginning to sting from looking at a screen for so long. About to stop and have a break, she decided to give it just a few more minutes. She continued tapping…

And suddenly, her screen changed.

"Oh my God." Evie sucked in a shaky breath. "I'm in!"

The words sounded surreal coming out of her mouth. After working on the damn thing for almost a year, the file consuming her every thought and action, it finally sat in front of her eyes, open.

Immediately stopping what he was doing, Wyatt looked at her screen. Pulling a phone out of his pocket, he typed something quickly before putting it away.

Gently brushing Evie's hands from her laptop, Wyatt reached over and pulled it in front of him. There were dozens of additional folders within, each bearing a name.

The door to the room opened, and all seven men walked in, including one hazel-eyed man who Evie hadn't met before. Oliver. It had to be. The last member of the team.

Wyatt looked up at his team, excitement on his face. "Evie got us in."

Glancing at the men, she saw a mixture of shocked and relieved expressions.

Eden spoke first. "What's in there?"

Wyatt's gaze skimmed the folders. "Files with names. I recognize some of them. Doctors we met. Other SEALs and soldiers. This first file just says Project Arma." He clicked into it, and Evie recognized the document immediately. It was the one that had sat open on Troy's laptop. "The doc labeled Project Arma just seems to have a brief description of the program with a list of names." Wyatt looked up. "Looks like file names...and we each have one."

Wyatt's eyes continued to search the screen—then he stopped and turned to Evie.

Dread pooled in her stomach. She already suspected what he was going to say but prayed she was wrong.

"You have a file too, Evie."

Her throat constricted. What the hell? Why did she have a

file? She only knew about the project from snooping in Troy's office.

Luca walked closer and placed his hand on Evie's shoulder, giving her the strength she needed. "Open it."

Wyatt raised his brows but said nothing. Turning back to the laptop, he clicked on the file with her name. When it popped open, Evie leaned closer.

Staring back from the screen were her own green eyes, next to what appeared to be her bio. What the hell? The image was a high school headshot.

Wyatt, Luca, and Evie leaned in, all reading the information.

No. It couldn't be possible.

A mixture of rage and shock filled her.

"It was all a lie..." The words left Evie in a whisper. Luca's thumb began to stroke her shoulder in support.

"What was a lie?" It was Asher who asked the question.

Evie couldn't speak, rage and resentment clouding her thoughts.

Luca answered. "According to this, they targeted Evie since high school and wanted to recruit her for her IT skills. Troy was assigned to watch her and eventually bring her in."

Clenching her jaw, Evie felt bile rising in her stomach. She was used. Completely. *Everything* had been a setup. And she'd fallen for all of it.

"Why did he never bring her in then?" Mason asked.

Luca glanced down at Evie, and their gazes held. "Maybe he decided he didn't want to let her go?"

Evie's heart raced. Was that it? Had the people running Project Arma told Troy to get close, only to have him decide he was going to keep her indefinitely?

Her skin chilled.

"They wouldn't have agreed to that," Wyatt said, finally drawing his gaze away from the screen.

"Maybe he didn't give them a choice. He wasn't himself in the end. Who knows what he was willing to risk to keep her."

Evie's body was fighting between heartbreak and anger. "Was my whole life just a game for them to play as they pleased? Did I even get a choice in any of it?"

Fury tore through her. Who the hell did these people think they were? Who did *Troy* think he was? Dating her because someone ordered him to, then keeping her like she was a damn toy! She was so sick of being manipulated and used.

Luca crouched down so he was eye level with Evie. "I know, sweetheart. I'm sorry."

Sick of being the victim, Evie clenched her fists. "I hope he *does* come after me. I hope we find him—and he gets what he deserves."

Evie saw the glint in Luca's eyes. "He will."

"We'll make sure of it."

Eden's voice pulled Evie's gaze up. All seven men looked just as enraged as Luca.

Oddly, her own anger lifted slightly at the sight, and she felt touched by the men's reactions. She may have felt like she had no family a month ago, but she sure didn't feel like that now.

CHAPTER 25

*L*UCA SKIMMED the list of names. So many people that he had trusted, said hello to every day. They'd all known. They had been part of the big cover-up that made Luca and dozens of others unknowing and non-consensual test subjects.

"Does Shylah have a folder?"

Luca tore his attention from the screen to look up at Eden.

Wyatt skimmed through the list until he hovered over a name. "Yeah, she does, Hunter."

Eden's expression didn't change. Luca had always held out hope for Eden that Shylah was innocent in the whole project. Had hoped that she'd been as unaware as them.

"Having a file doesn't mean she had a hand in what was going on, Eden. I had one, and I didn't."

Eden glanced at Evie as she spoke the words, hope in his eyes before he quickly masked all emotion. "She knew. I'll look through it later. I'm going to get some work done." Eden turned and walked away.

Placing his hand on Evie's shoulder, Luca gave a light squeeze. A silent thank you for trying to help. Eden's struggle since Shylah disappeared after the project was uncovered had been eating away at his friend ever since.

"I think Evie and I will head home now," Luca said, glancing up at his team. He could sense that Evie's mood was low after the information she had learned. Hell, he didn't blame her. Who wanted to find out they were a pawn piece in someone else's game?

Evie glanced up at Luca. "Don't you want to look at the files?"

"There's plenty of time for that." When she looked like she wanted to argue the point, Luca took her hand and pulled her up. "Let's walk. It will be good for you to get some fresh air after sitting in front of a screen all day."

Not questioning him, Evie stood and turned to go. Wyatt's hand on her arm halted her. "Well done today, Ace."

"Ace?" Luca smiled.

"She's part of the team now, so she needs a team name, doesn't she?"

Evie flushed. Luca pulled her into his side and placed a kiss on her cheek, feeling grateful that his brothers now saw her as he did.

"See you guys tomorrow. Keep me updated if you find anything important."

Walking out, they said goodbye to Lexie before making it to the street.

Strolling in silence, Luca placed his arm around Evie's waist and studied his surroundings. Troy could be anywhere and could pop up any time. Luca was ready. So ready. He needed Troy to be caught so he could breathe easier, knowing she wasn't at risk every minute of the day.

Sliding into the car, Luca drove them back to his house. Over the drive, he noticed that Evie appeared thoughtful. He remained quiet, knowing she would talk when she was ready.

"I should probably be moving back to my place soon."

Wanting to laugh, Luca shook his head. "Oh, darlin', I'm not letting you out of my sight."

Expecting an argument, Luca was surprised when Evie breathed out a sigh of relief. "Good, because I don't really *want* to move back."

This time Luca did laugh. "Why suggest it then?"

She lifted her shoulders. "I don't want you to feel trapped with me, Luca. If you're with me, I want it to be because you want to be. Not because you have to protect me."

Reaching out his hand, Luca squeezed her leg. "Evie, I've wanted you since the first day I laid eyes on you. I don't know what it was, but something about you just pulled me in. Then I got to know you. Safe to say I'm not going anywhere. I'll be around until you're sick of me."

"I can't see that happening."

"Good." Taking her hand in his, he raised it to his lips and pressed a kiss to her warm skin. "Because even if you *did* get sick of me, sweetheart, I'd still be at your door until you took me back."

That was the damn truth.

They made the rest of the drive home in silence. When Evie disappeared into the bedroom to get changed, Luca whipped out his phone and dialed Asher's number.

"Man, are you missing me already?"

"I need a favor," Luca said.

"Hit me with it."

Luca quickly explained what he needed before hanging up. Evie had been through a lot. Too damn much. And their relationship hadn't had enough fun. Luca wanted to bring some of that back.

Walking into the bedroom, he noticed Evie staring at herself in the mirror. Standing behind her, he wrapped both arms around her waist, noting their significant size difference. He didn't know how any man could lay a violent hand on someone so fragile.

"What's on your mind?"

Their gazes met in the reflection. "I just...I thought I would feel better once I opened the file. Once I had answers."

"You will, sweetheart. It will take time."

"How did you recover from knowing what they did to you?"

"I haven't. But knowing that every day the team and I get closer to bringing down the people who worked on the project helps." Evie nodded, but her expression still held sadness. "Why don't you take a bath, and I'll prepare dinner."

Eyes softening, Evie sank into him further. "You're too good to me, Luca."

"I'm trying to entice you into never leaving me, sweetheart. It's actually quite selfish, trust me." Placing a kiss on her forehead, Luca left the bedroom. Moving through the house, he gathered the things he needed and started preparing for their dinner.

Twenty minutes later, his phone buzzed, and he opened the door to find Asher there with a bag.

"Don't say I never do anything for you, buddy."

Once Luca took the bag, Asher was gone as quickly as he'd arrived. Shutting the door, Luca busied himself setting up their meal.

When he heard Evie getting out of the bath, he went up to the bedroom. Standing in the doorway, he crossed his arms and watched her.

God, but she was gorgeous.

Evie moved across the room to get dressed, looking so much happier than the girl he'd met all those weeks ago, despite the revelations of this afternoon. Luca was going to make damn sure it stayed that way. "You're so damn beautiful."

Evie's gaze clashed with Luca's for a moment, and heat worked its way up her neck. Pulling the top over her head, she walked toward him now fully dressed. "I hear that's a common line when a man sees a woman naked."

"You're dressed now, and you're still the most beautiful woman I've ever laid eyes on."

The smile that touched Evie's lips made Luca want to crush them with his own. "Dinner's ready, sweetheart. Let's get out of this room before I ruin my own plans."

"Good, I'm starving. Finding out you were wanted by a top-secret, non-sanctioned government project really works up an appetite."

Luca growled.

She smirked. "Sorry, too soon." Following Luca downstairs and to the back door, she hesitated. "Where are we going?"

"See for yourself." Opening the back door, Luca watched as Evie stepped out and smiled.

In the backyard, he'd set up a picnic with all the trimmings. On top of a blanket lay a dozen different foods accompanied by wine and candles.

"Can't let my hungry brainiac girlfriend starve, can I?"

Turning, Evie wrapped her arms around his middle. "What did I do to deserve you?"

"I ask myself that every day."

Giving Luca a light smack on the arm, Evie turned to face the picnic blanket. "You even brought music out here," she said, crouching by the Bluetooth speaker.

"Darlin', when I do something, I go all the way." Reaching into his pocket, Luca pulled out his phone to choose a playlist. "Although Asher did help me get the goods. But being my idea, I think I still get all the credit."

"I'll have to remember to thank him." Picking up a carrot stick, Evie watched as Luca lowered himself next to her on the blanket. "So, Mr. Perfect, you know all about me, now. Tell me something about you. Why did you become a SEAL?"

Opening a beer, Luca took a drink before answering the question. "Not an amazing story. I was twelve when I read about what a SEAL was. It was in some magazine my dad left lying around the house. It explained what they did and had pictures of these badass-looking guys. In the eyes of a twelve-year-old, it seemed like a pretty awesome job. I remember walking up to my parents and telling them that I was going to be a SEAL. My dad sat me down and told me that it would take hard work, and it wasn't an easy job, but if that's what I wanted to do, then that's what I would do."

"How did your mom react?"

"She wasn't so thrilled. She would have loved for me to get some safe office job."

Scrunching up her nose, Evie frowned. "I can't picture you in an office job."

"Never would have happened."

A small smile touched her lips. "Are they good people? Your parents?"

Luca didn't have to think about it. "The best, and they're going to love you. I mean, don't get me wrong, if you get stuck in a conversation with them, you're their hostage for a good couple of hours, and they play Elton John like there's no tomorrow, but you can't help but love them."

Evie's eyes grew cloudy. "I hope I can meet them someday."

"You will." He would introduce them tomorrow if he could. That's how damn sure he was about Evie. Moving a piece of hair behind her ear, he leaned in and placed a kiss on her head.

"So, was he right?"

Lost for a moment, Luca frowned. "Who?"

"Your dad. Was it hard work? Was the job not so easy?"

A laugh escaped Luca's chest as he pictured his all-knowing dad. "My father is never wrong. The job *was* hard. The training we had to go through was the most physically and mentally exhausting experience of my life, but I figured out pretty early that you can get through almost anything if you know the pain's temporary. Wouldn't change a thing. Being a SEAL meant I got to help a lot of people, and it gave me the skills and discipline to set up the business so the guys and I can *continue* helping people. Also, I met my team, my brothers. We keep each other alive, keep each other sane. The biggest thing the Navy ever gave me was them, my family."

"That's really nice, Luca. How come you didn't remain a SEAL?"

He sighed. "After the facility was raided, we were told the truth and given a choice to stay or go. We were *so* angry. We knew we couldn't stay. We still wanted to help people with the skills we'd acquired but we wanted to do it on our terms. We did agree to help the CIA locate the rest of the Project Arma staff, though. We also agreed to keep what happened a secret."

Luca knew it was only to avoid the media frenzy the team could have started.

"What you've built in Marble Protection is amazing."

He definitely thought so.

"Thank you, darlin'." Fixing himself a plate, Luca decided he *did* owe Asher. The guy chose great picnic food. "Enough about me. Tell me…do you want to go back and finish school?"

Evie gazed at the gray clouds in the sky, looking pensive. For a moment, he thought she wasn't going to answer. "I think I would just like some time to get to know myself again. I feel like I've either been a victim or a girl on the run most of my adult life. After we catch Troy, it would be nice just to be Evie for a bit, then maybe pick up my studies again."

"That sounds like a good plan, and please know that I'll be right here for you for whatever you need."

Evie opened her mouth to say something just as his phone buzzed. Glancing down, he saw Mason's name flash across the screen.

"Hey, Eagle, can I call you back?" Luca said as he picked up.

There was static and buzzing across the line, and Luca struggled to make out what Mason was saying. *Damn reception.*

Grabbing Evie's hand, Luca pulled her up so they could walk inside. Once there, he went into the living room so he could hear his friend clearly.

He quietly sighed, hating that the call was interrupting their date, but knowing his friend wouldn't interrupt without good reason.

CHAPTER 26

*G*LANCING OUT THE window, Evie took in the gray clouds suddenly moving in. It was going to rain at any moment. When she glanced down again, she spotted Misty on the rug.

There you are, honey.

Misty hadn't come by the last few days and Evie had been getting worried.

When Misty moved over the rug, Evie leaned forward. Was she limping?

Not only that, but she was also heading right for the candle.

Turning back to Luca, she saw him still talking to Mason— and whatever they were discussing had Luca looking enraged. Cringing as a shiver ran down her back, she pitied whoever that look was aimed at.

When she looked back again, Misty was putting her nose up to the flame.

No!

Dashing out the back door, she felt raindrops touch her shoulders as she quickly jogged over to the blanket— then stopped short.

Misty was gone.

A chill that had nothing to do with the rain seeped into Evie's bones. Had Misty run into the woods? She'd only looked away for seconds before coming outside…

Glancing at the house, she saw Luca's face through the window.

His eyes appeared wide with fear, his body frozen in place.

Evie's stomach dropped. *Nothing* scared Luca.

As she took a step closer to the house, he disappeared. He moved so quickly it was like he vanished into thin air.

Her mind screamed *run*, right as a hand covered her mouth. Her body was thrown over a hard shoulder as strong arms restrained her legs.

When her injured ribs clashed with a rock-solid shoulder, pain stole her breath.

Before she could catch it again, he started moving through the woods at an unimaginable speed. Evie tried to keep the nausea rising up her throat at bay.

Struggling to comprehend what was happening, she attempted to use both hands to push up and take some of the pressure off her healing ribs. It was no use. Every time she was able to gain an inch, she was jolted and lost her grasp.

Instead, Evie focused on her breathing. The one thing she could control. The chance of passing out from the pain or throwing up from the motion seemed very likely at that moment, and neither option was particularly appealing.

After what felt like forever but was more likely just minutes, the person stopped moving. Evie heard something creak open, then brief weightlessness as they both dropped down into a dark hole.

The pain to her ribs upon landing was like nothing she'd felt before. She was dumped to the ground, her hip and shoulder colliding with the earth, causing her to cry out in pain.

A hand immediately latched onto her throat and she was

pulled to her feet. Evie's vision blurred as her body was shoved hard against a wall.

Blinking several times before her eyes would focus, Evie felt everything inside her freeze when she eventually made out the person holding her. In front of her stood the man she hoped to never see again.

Troy.

And behind him stood the man who had just snatched her.

"Thanks, I owe you one. Cover the entrance before you go."

The man nodded, before jumping up into what looked like a trap door and closing it behind him.

As reality hit, the pain in her body faded to the background. Everything disappeared around her and a buzzing started in her ears.

He looked exactly the same. It was like she'd been thrust back in time a year, staring at the devil himself again.

"Remember me, Evaline?" The acid stench of his breath gagged her as he spat the words at her face. "The man you ran from like a fucking *coward*?"

Shouting the last word, he again slammed her body into the wall. The debilitating fear cascading through her dulled the pain.

She attempted to make her voice work, but no words came out. The desire to lash out and fight back at the monster who'd tormented her was intense.

She wanted to scream at him to get away from her. To go to hell. But the fear was like a thick fog that clouded her brain and stole her voice. Her body felt paralyzed. All the times he'd scared her to the brink of insanity flashed through her mind.

Troy's fingers tightened on her throat, and panic started to build as her air was cut off. Just as black spots entered her vision, her body flew across the room before hitting another wall at full force. Crumpling to the ground, she saw bright red blood dripping from somewhere on her head, sinking into the hard-packed earth.

"It's like old times, isn't it? You disobeying me, me having to discipline you."

Glancing around, Evie tried to figure out where he'd taken her. It was a tiny, cold room that smelled of the earth. The air was muggy and damp.

An old military bunker, maybe?

The only light came from a small lantern.

A small mattress, a round table with a couple of chairs, and some kitchen supplies were the only items within view. Had Troy been living here?

Turning her attention back to him, she saw the smug look on his face. Anger rose inside of her like a wave.

Who did he think he was? What gave him the right to believe he could just take her and treat her as he wished? It was *her* body he was abusing. *Her* life he was interfering with.

"Fuck you, Troy."

The laugh that escaped him was pure evil. "Oh, the mouse has a voice now, does she?"

Troy was across the space in a blink, fisting his fingers in her hair, causing Evie to cry out. The pain of hair being ripped from her scalp radiated through her head.

"You haven't been very good, have you, darling? What am I going to do with you?" Troy's nose lowered to her neck, and she had to stop herself from gagging. "You still smell the same. God, I've missed you. I've been watching, though."

More black dots entered Evie's peripheral. She blinked a few times, refusing to give in to the darkness.

"Why?" The word came out as a gasp.

With his hand still holding her hair in a tight grip, Troy used the other to trail a finger down the side of her face. "What? You thought I wouldn't come for you? Oh, Evaline, you really are a dumb bitch." His head lowered, a mere inch separating their faces. "Don't you get it? You *belong* to me—and I keep what's mine."

198

Heart lurching, Evie thought it might beat right out of her chest.

Closing her eyes, she took deep breaths as she pictured Luca. Sweet Luca. He would find her. He had to. Opening her eyes, she focused her steely gaze on Troy. "Luca's going to come, you know. He'll find me. And he'll destroy you."

Pushing Evie to the ground, Troy almost looked pleased by that. "I'm counting on it."

Gathering as much strength as possible, she pushed herself into a sitting position against the wall. "What are you talking about?"

Turning, he picked up a gun from the table and began loading it with bullets.

"Luca was always the favorite. Him and his whole damn team of golden boys. I *told* them Luca's team would never agree to fight for them. Carry out their missions. Do you think they listened? Stupid assholes. But Luca's too valuable. Too strong and fast. They didn't want to end him like they should have. I knew what had to be done then, and I still do. That's why I'm here, Evie. For you—but also for them."

A shiver ran up her spine. Was the project still running?

Before she could think more about it, Troy continued. "In all the time I've known Luca, he's never had a weakness. And now he does. This will be a two-for-one."

It was her. Troy knew Evie was Luca's weakness. Trying to bury the instant guilt, Evie asked, "Why Luca?"

Troy shook his head. "Luca's just the start. Once he's out of the picture, we'll pick them off one by one. They'll begin to fall apart once the first person in their team dies. Then they'll drop like flies."

Evie's eyes widened. "We?"

Troy banged the gun down on the small table, causing her to jump. "Stop being so fucking stupid, Evie! Do you really think Luca's the only one who still has a team? God!" His expression turned sly. "They wanted to recruit you too, you know. I convinced them you weren't Project Arma material. It wasn't hard, especially after I encouraged you to drop out of college. Then you were mine to keep forever."

Glancing at Troy, she wondered how she ever missed the pure evil that existed inside him.

Knowing she had to ask, dreading it, she voiced the question that had been on her mind for so long. "Did you kill my parents?"

"Of course I did. They were making too much noise about you. They didn't give me a choice."

Unbearable pain shot through her. She'd known it was true. Felt it. But hearing the words come out of his mouth was more horrible than she'd anticipated.

Going still, Troy suddenly gazed toward the roof. He grinned at Evie, excitement shining in his eyes, the sight filling her with dread. "It's go time."

Reaching across the table, Troy grabbed a gas mask. Opening a box, he pulled out two small bottles, each with a nozzle.

Evie's heart accelerated. "What are you doing? What are those?"

Troy's smile grew. "This is how we catch lover boy, my darling Evaline."

He donned the mask before affixing the bottles on either side of what appeared to be a trap door on the low roof.

That's when it hit Evie. "You're going to gas us?"

"Not enough to kill you. That wouldn't be any fun. I'll wait until you wake up, so you can watch while I kill *him*. Nice and slow." Then he reached for her. "Time to make you scream so golden boy comes running."

Fighting off sheer panic, she vowed not to make a sound. She wouldn't let Luca step into a trap. Wouldn't get anyone else killed.

Troy grabbed a fistful of her hair, and she gritted her teeth to stop from shouting out in pain. His fist came fast and hard and would have knocked her across the room, if Troy didn't have such a tight hold on her hair.

Evie dug her nails into his hand, breaking the skin, clawing at the hand that held her. The pain in her scalp and face was unbearable.

His knee flew up, hitting her in the ribs, right where they were already cracked. Biting her bottom lip and tasting blood, she still refused to make a sound, even as each breath sent shooting pains down her body. She prayed he would go too far and the darkness would take her.

As Troy pressed her against the wall with his body, something Luca had said replayed in her head…

You can get through almost anything if you know the pain's temporary.

This is temporary pain, Evie. Get through it. Save Luca.

Another punch hit Evie in the ribs, stealing the breath from her body.

That's when she realized it wasn't just her screams Luca would be able to hear…

As another knee landed in Evie's middle, she called on all her strength. Taking a big breath before yelling out as loudly as possible.

"Don't come down here, Luca! It's a trap! There's gas. Get away!"

As the last word left Evie's lips, the roof opened and Luca dropped down.

CHAPTER 27

$\mathcal{E}$VIE'S VOICE CUT through the silence. Luca didn't think. He just moved.

His team would have his ass for not waiting for them, but Evie's voice sounded full of pure torment, and he sure as hell wasn't going to stand around and wait.

Her scream was something about gas and a trap, but he didn't care. He wouldn't leave her in the company of Troy any longer than necessary. He wouldn't have been able to stop himself from getting to her even if he tried.

Having already spotted the difference in the ground surface, Luca didn't hesitate. He scrambled for the edge of the false ground, wrenching open a camouflaged door and dropping into the hole.

Immediately, gas hissed into Luca's face, triggered by the door opening. His lungs started to compress as he landed on his feet, stumbling back a step.

Before he could recover, a fist came out of nowhere, his reflexes too slow to stop it. The combination of the hit and the gas smashed Luca into the wall behind him. The fist quickly returned again and again, hitting him in the ribs, then the gut.

The little remaining air was knocked out of his lungs. The punches kept coming, but his own body seemed to be moving in slow motion, unable to defend itself.

From the corner of his eye, Luca noticed a limp body on the ground. So still, the person hardly seemed alive. Golden-brown hair tinged with bright red blood.

Evie.

A ferocious anger filled him. Troy had hurt his woman —again.

Pushing to the back of his mind how still her body appeared, and what that meant, Luca forced himself to move past the pain, dodging the next fist.

Lifting his leg, he swiftly kicked the body in front of him, stumbling forward. Luca noticed the effects of the gas were already starting to pass, his breaths coming easier.

"What the hell?" Troy's voice was full of shock and outrage. "There's enough gas to knock your ass unconscious!"

"You underestimated me, asshole."

Troy swung at Luca's face. This time, Luca caught the fist easily. Pivoting and placing his body between Evie's unconscious form and Troy, Luca twisted the arm until he heard a crack. Troy screamed in pain.

"What did you do to her?" Luca demanded.

The pain faded from Troy's expression, changing to one of sadistic pleasure. "Nothing that I haven't done before."

Luca saw red. Only his years of training prevented him from immediately lashing out at the man. He had to wait for the gas to leave his system, or Troy would have the upper hand.

Troy ripped the mask off his face, blinking when the gas had little effect. "Well, look at that. Our bodies are practically indestructible!" Troy's laugh made Luca want to rip his throat out. "And this is what you're fighting against? The people who gave this to us? This was a *gift*!" He yelled the last word, and Luca wondered if Troy was, in fact, insane. "No one can stop us now!"

"I don't know about you, but I prefer to control what goes into my body. And just so you're aware, I'm gonna fucking destroy you."

"You're a joke, you know that?" Troy sneered with derision. "I told them. I told them so many damn times that you weren't up for the job. And they wouldn't listen to me!"

Luca tried to tune out Troy's rant and listen for Evie's heart rate, but the fading gas in his body was still hindering his abilities. He had to stall a bit longer. "So what's the plan? Kill me, take Evie and run?" Not that it would ever happen. Evie was never leaving his sight again.

"Kill you, yes. Take Evie, yes...but not to where you might think."

Moving half a step back toward Evie, Luca retorted, "What's the harm in telling me, Troy? I mean, if I'm going to be dead anyway. Unless you don't actually think you can kill me. Are *you* not up for the job?"

Troy's fists clenched. "Project Arma can only survive if no one's hunting us. Killing your team is a no-brainer. We would've done it on your last SEAL mission, but you weren't in the goddamn building when it exploded! Then the project was infiltrated, and we had to abort the mission and go into hiding. I wanted to get on with the job, but my team said no."

Luca frowned. "The mission?"

Troy's smile was slow, chilling. "You thought it was over? You have no idea. This is a lot bigger than you could ever imagine."

Blood boiling, Luca took a step forward. "Where are the rest of them?"

"You won't find them. They're so deep in hiding, they'll only be found if they wish to be. They're more powerful than you know. You'll be dead anyway...and sweet Evie over there will be with me. I was too lenient on her before. This time, I'll make sure she fears the very *thought* of escaping—" He stopped, his eyes narrowing at the sound of distant footsteps moving at a high rate of speed. Whoever it was, they wouldn't be long.

"Time to end this shit," Troy muttered.

He lunged for a gun on the small table.

Before his hand could wrap around the weapon, Luca was there, his body slamming into Troy at full force.

On impact, both men hit the ground hard, the table crashing and the gun spinning before landing feet away. The first to recover, Luca threw a punch before easily dodging a kick to the gut.

Hearing a whimper from Evie, Luca swung his head around, costing him precious focus. Troy took advantage, releasing a kick that knocked Luca to the ground.

Rolling into a crouch, he saw Troy reach into his back pocket and whip out a knife. He slashed out, the blade catching Luca's shirt, barely missing his skin. Moving faster than Troy could track, Luca seized his wrist and swiped the knife from his fingers. He plunged it into the other man's thigh.

Troy's face creased with rage and pain as he howled. "You fucking bastard!"

"Guess I got the upgraded version of the drug, Troy."

"I'm going to kill you!"

Luca grabbed Troy's foot as he dove for the gun, slamming him to the ground just before he reached it. Climbing on top of Troy, Luca swung. Fast. Hard.

They thrashed on the ground, both getting in hits, Luca avoiding as many as possible.

Finally gaining the upper hand, Luca ruthlessly dug his fingers into the knife wound.

Troy let out a shriek that quickly morphed into a deranged laugh. His expression was nothing short of psychotic. "You should have heard her scream. She was so sure you'd save her— and *look* at her. Unconscious in the corner. Broken. I don't even know if she's alive."

Fury vibrated through Luca's chest as he pummeled Troy to within an inch of his life.

When Luca heard shallow gasps coming from below him, he forced himself to stop. He needed to keep Troy alive. He had information.

Face bloodied, Troy stared at Luca, his eyes mere slits. "You think this stops with me? This is the beginning of the end for all of you." The laugh that escaped his lips crackled with the wet sound of blood in his throat. "You won't kill me. I'm too valuable to you. I'll escape eventually, and when I do, that sweet piece of ass in the corner is coming with me. She'll never see the light of day again."

Luca didn't hesitate. His hands flew to Troy's neck and he twisted, snapping the bones in less than a second.

The life left Troy's eyes as his body went limp.

Not sparing him a second thought, Luca jumped to his feet just as Eden dropped down into the room. He moved quickly to Evie, dropping to his knees, his fingers gently probing her throat. It was faint, but he felt a pulse.

"I was closest. The rest of the guys shouldn't be far off." Eden's voice cut through the silence. "You killed him."

Luca felt no remorse. "He didn't leave me a choice."

Slowly approaching, Eden put a hand on his shoulder. "Good. I'm glad the asshole's dead."

Wrapping his arms around Evie's still body, Luca stood. "Let's go."

"You're injured. Want me to take her?"

"No. Let's go."

Moving up a rickety ladder, Luca was able to clutch Evie to his chest with one arm and climb with the other. His body was regaining its strength, as well as his other abilities. The light fluttering of Evie's heart calmed some of the turmoil inside him.

Once they were at ground level, Eden and Luca both moved

swiftly through the trees. They made it to Luca's house in minutes. Once there, Luca climbed into the back of the car while Eden got behind the wheel.

As they drove away, Eden placed a call. "Rocket and I are headed to the hospital. Evie's hurt but alive. Just. We need you to pick up Troy from the woods behind Rocket's house. He's about two miles east of the house in an underground military bunker."

"Dead or alive?" Wyatt's voice was all business.

"Dead."

There was a slight pause. "Got it."

The line went dead as Eden focused on the road once more.

"We got the fire at Marble Protection put out. Had to call the fire department, and Lexie was almost caught in it. Asher got her out. The office and a few other rooms have fire damage."

In everything that had happened, Luca had forgotten about the call from Mason, telling him about the fire. Without taking his eyes from Evie, Luca asked, "Any idea how it started?"

Eden's voice was hard. "Looks like it originated in the office. Wyatt was able to recover data from the cameras. Someone in a black hoodie came in while Lexie was in the restroom. They went straight to the office and lit a fire using paper and gasoline. Couldn't see his face but he was definitely moving fast enough."

"Had to be one of the guys from Troy's SEAL team. Alistair is definitely in on this. He was the one who took Evie from my lawn."

Alistair was one of the seven men from Troy's team. If Luca hadn't wanted to murder them before, he sure did now.

Pushing a lock of Evie's hair off her face, Luca noted her skin was already deepening to various shades of black and purple. Anger came back tenfold as his muscles clenched. If Luca could, he would kill Troy all over again. "It was a distraction. To get me away from Evie just long enough for him to take her."

Eden nodded his confirmation.

Tuning into Evie's body, Luca listened to her heartbeat. It was slow. Too slow. "Hurry, Hunter. She needs medical attention. Now."

CHAPTER 28

*E*VIE'S EYES FLICKERED open, and she had to stop a groan at the familiar pain in her ribs. As her gaze darted around the room, she realized she was in a hospital bed—again.

She took a calming breath as the memories rushed back. Troy had taken her. Threatened her. Threatened Luca. Did the fact she was in a hospital bed mean Luca had saved her? Where was he?

She spotted the empty chair close to her bed.

He was here, somewhere. The man was indestructible.

A light breeze had Evie turning her head. Noticing the open window, she frowned. Had the nurses opened it?

Carefully crawling out of bed, Evie tested her balance as she stood. Her legs wobbled, but when she didn't pass out, she took that as a good sign.

Slowly moving toward the window, she stopped when she caught a strange smell.

Was that gas?

She turned toward the door—and cried out abruptly when someone grabbed her from behind, placing an arm around her neck.

"We meet at last, Evie. I've heard so much about you." The voice was unfamiliar.

Only just reaching the ground with her toes, she knew the huge arm would choke her if the man wrenched her any higher.

She didn't have to wait long for help. With a bang, her hospital door flew open and Luca was there, holding a gun. Mason and Eden were behind him.

"Get the fuck off her." Luca's voice was flat. Deadly.

Two more men stepped out of the bathroom. Neither was armed, but both looked very capable of holding their own in a fight.

"Luca, so good to see you, old friend. I'd put that gun down if I were you." She felt him nod toward something in the corner. "Don't tell me you can't smell that. It's natural gas. When mixed with a bullet… Well, you can imagine, right?"

"Boom," one of the other men said in an excited tone.

Evie's heart sped up. Were they saying there could be an explosion?

Luca's eyes hardened, but other than that, his expression didn't change.

"Don't believe me? By all means, give it a go. We'll probably get out in time, you know, with our speed and all, but poor Evie here won't be so lucky."

She whimpered as the arm around her neck tightened slightly, and she was pulled further onto her toes.

Luca let out a growl. Then his hand dropped, placing the gun somewhere at his back. Mason and Eden did the same. "If you don't loosen your damn grip, I'm going to end you right the fuck now." When the arm holding her loosened slightly, Luca continued. "Tell me what the fuck you want, Carter."

"So the rumors are true. You *do* have a soft spot now." The man chuckled like he was talking to a friend. "We're just here to send a little message to you and your boys."

As the smell of gas became stronger, Evie's head felt cloudy.

She pushed herself to stay conscious, using every bit of strength she could muster.

"I had no idea that Troy was here, and I only just found out a couple of my guys helped him. They'll be dealt with. I take no responsibility for what happened here. But you *are* getting too close. So either join us—or leave us alone."

"Us?"

"We know you're aware, Luca. The project is still very much alive. It was always too big for the government to think it could just shut us down. You want out? Fine. But stay the hell away from us. Got it?"

Evie could see Luca's fists clench as the veins popped out on his arms.

Mason stepped forward. "If we refuse?"

Evie's breath was cut off as the arm tightened to an unbearable degree. "Watch what the consequences are."

In the blink of an eye, all hell broke loose. Luca moved before anyone could stop him and lunged for the man holding Evie. She stumbled as he released her, but her fall was cushioned by Luca, who seemed to be everywhere at once. Gently placing her on the floor, he swiveled in his crouched position.

Mason and Eden had moved toward the other men, throwing blows that would make the toughest man fall.

As Luca sprang forward, he blocked her view, but she could still see some of the blows he dealt the man who'd held her, Carter, as they fought.

She shrank into the corner, the violence causing her stomach to contract. All the men in the room were deadly. Not one of them showed an ounce of emotion. They moved like machines.

When the man fighting Luca produced a knife, Evie tried to stand up. "Luca!"

"Stay the hell back, Evie!"

She stilled at his command. Not sure her legs would hold her much longer, she wrapped her arms around herself and prayed for it all to end.

As the knife flew toward Luca's shoulder, he dodged it easily. Doing some defensive maneuver that Evie had only seen in movies, he knocked the blade from the man's hand.

Now without a weapon, the man leapt onto the windowsill, appearing more animal than human. Turning back, he glared. "Remember what I said, Luca."

Then the man dropped from the third-floor window.

Evie's eyes widened. Surely he wouldn't survive a drop that high.

Before she could process it further, the other two men maneuvered themselves away from Mason and Eden and followed suit, diving after Carter.

Evie's breaths were pained. She slowly slid down the wall, back to the floor.

Luca crouched in front of her, trepidation in his eyes. Reaching for her but stopping short, he spoke softly, as if anything loud might startle her. "Are you okay, sweetheart?"

Evie nodded, waiting for him to touch her. When he didn't, she tried to get up, but realized her body felt too heavy from the adrenaline.

"Be still. I won't come closer. I'm sorry you had to see that."

Evie's mind reeled. Why wouldn't he come closer? If he wouldn't come to her, she'd *force* her body to move. Pushing herself off the floor, Evie groaned at the pain she felt everywhere. It was like she had been injured so grievously, her body felt like it was collapsing from the inside.

Luca was beside her in a flash, gingerly placing his arm around her. Evie clung to him. Didn't want to risk him moving away once she was steady.

When he attempted to pull back, Evie's tenacious fingers tightened.

"I thought you would want…space. After what you just saw us do."

He thought she would want space from *him*? Hell no. "I need to be close to you, Luca. It's the only place I feel safe."

Groaning, he pulled Evie into his arms. She pressed her face to his chest and breathed him in. Luca held most of her weight as she leaned against him. She vaguely heard Luca talking to the guys, but didn't listen to what they were saying. She was too exhausted, too overwrought.

Sweeping Evie into his strong arms, Luca walked back to the bed as she continued to breathe him in. Luca was her safety net. Her home.

Then her eyes popped open as she was jolted by the memory of why she was here. "Troy—"

"You're safe, sweetheart. Troy won't be bothering you ever again."

Ever again. She wasn't sure if she was supposed to feel some sort of guilt at the meaning behind Luca's words, but she couldn't muster any emotion other than relief. Was she really safe? Could she stop running?

Resting her head against Luca's chest, Evie allowed her body to relax, refusing to think about the answers to those questions. Closing her eyes, she simply let the warmth of Luca's body warm her own.

As afternoon light flooded the room, Evie's eyes opened. Sitting up slowly, she glanced at the painkillers sitting next to a glass of water on Luca's bedside table. Reaching for the pills, she swallowed them without hesitating.

Carefully climbing out of bed, she felt stiff and sore, but it was nothing she couldn't handle.

Hearing male voices downstairs, Evie nibbled her lip, wondering whether she should head down.

Stop being a wimp, she scolded herself. *You're a part of this as much as they are.*

Throwing on some clothes first, which was quite an effort in her current state, Evie headed for the living room.

At the sight of eight deadly SEALs scattered around the space, she stopped. Some wore scowls on their faces, some just had narrowed eyes, but the anger was easy to read in each of them. The intensity of their fury made the air feel thick and heavy.

Wanting to turn back and hide in the bedroom, Evie almost did exactly that. Before she could consider it further, Luca stood from the couch, moving to her side. Placing a kiss on her cheek, he snaked his arm around her waist. Evie leaned into him, absorbing his strength.

"What are you doing out of bed, sweetheart?"

She shrugged. "I heard voices."

"How are you feeling, Ace?"

Evie met Wyatt's gaze and a hint of a smile touched her lips. "I've had better days, but I'll be all right."

Giving her a nod, Wyatt returned the smile. "I'm glad to see you're doing okay."

"We all are," Eden added. His voice was deep, steeped with honesty and a hint of anger over what had happened to her.

Warmth filled Evie at the other men's murmurs of agreement.

Addressing the others, Wyatt gestured to the door with his head. "Let's get out of here."

Within minutes, the room had cleared and it was just Evie and Luca. Lifting her from her feet, he walked to the couch and sat with her on his lap.

"Luca, I can walk."

Dropping his face to her hair, he breathed deeply, remaining there while he spoke. "I need you in my arms. I came too damn close to losing you."

She caressed his chest with her hand. "I was so scared I wouldn't see you again."

"I swear to you, Evie, nothing like that will *ever* happen to you again."

"I love you, Luca." The words slipped from her lips. Part of her wished she could pull them back, but another part of her was relieved they were out in the open.

There was a moment of silence, during which she thought her heart might explode from her chest out of nerves. Then a smile stretched Luca's lips.

"I love you too, Evie. I've been wanting to say it for a while, but I didn't want to scare you off." He lowered his head and lightly touched his lips to hers. "God, I love you so much."

Evie hadn't felt this level of happiness in so long. Possibly ever. She knew Project Arma was still out there...but she didn't have to run and hide. She would make her stand here. She had friends, a town she enjoyed, and someone who loved her.

Not just someone—Luca.

"Move in with me."

Her gaze shot up to meet his. "You want me to move in with you? Permanently?" Was he serious? "What if you don't feel this way once everything has calmed down?"

"Darlin', what I feel is not temporary. Move in with me so when I wake up, you're the first thing I see every morning."

Tears pricked the back of her eyes. "You're too good to be true."

"Is that a yes?"

Feeling too emotional to speak, Evie nodded.

Luca pulled her head to his chest. "I have something else to ask you, too."

She raised her head again. She didn't know whether to be nervous or not.

"The guys and I think you're an amazing receptionist, but we're wondering if you would consider being our resident tech guru instead? Wyatt's been splitting time between three jobs. He wants to do more searching for Project Arma, and be more active at Marble Protection, so you would be freeing him up a lot. Plus, you're amazing." Luca reached for a pamphlet that sat on the coffee table and held it out to her. "I also found some great online tech courses you could take. If that's something you're still interested in doing?"

With tentative fingers, Evie took it from him. As she slowly leafed through the pamphlet, her emotions were all over the place.

"What do you think, sweetheart?"

"I'm scared that I'm going to wake up and be back to who I was a couple of months ago. I didn't know that I could ever feel this happy."

Running his knuckles down her cheek, Luca left a trail of warmth. "I hate that Troy made you believe you weren't deserving of happiness, Evie. You'll never feel that way again. Ever. Okay?"

Nodding, Evie moved her lips to Luca's. "I love you, Luca, so much."

"I love you too, sweetheart."

CHAPTER 29

*E*DEN SAT IN the booth at the back of the bar, watching the crowd.

It had been a month since things had gone down with Troy. Eden was glad the fucker was dead. He felt no remorse for the guy after what he'd done to Evie. What he'd done to her for years.

Anger boiled inside him at the thought of *any* man abusing a woman, much less a SEAL. Someone who was supposed to have honor. Someone whose strength rivaled that of most others. Troy was damn lucky he was dead, or Eden would have done the job himself.

Spotting Luca and Evie on the dance floor, he smirked at how out of time they were with the music. Their slow movements contradicted the up-tempo beat. They didn't seem to care in the least.

Evie had recovered well in the last month, but Eden knew from experience that the emotional recovery would take a lot longer. Luca would be there to help her along the way. He'd never seen his friend so happy.

Wanting to be happy *for* him, Eden took another swig of beer and tried to swallow his resentment.

Apparently, he was the only one who fell for women who lied and betrayed him.

Eden cast his gaze away from the happy couple, not wanting to be reminded of what he'd lost.

What a load of shit *that* was. He'd *never* had Shylah. She'd known about the project all along. There was no other explanation for her disappearance. She was working in the damn *medical* department. Sleeping with him at night and injecting him with experimental drugs during the day.

Eden's grip tightened on his beer. Not a day passed when he didn't think about her—and he *hated* himself for it.

He heard his team before he saw them. At least there were some benefits to being lied to about the shit being put into his body. Maybe he'd thank Shylah for his abilities if he ever found her. Too bad she'd dropped off the face of the planet.

Giving his friends a nod as they joined him in the booth, Eden kept his eyes downcast. Luca was still with Evie, but they all knew he would be listening from his spot on the dance floor.

Finally glancing up at his friends, Eden didn't mince his words. "You're late."

"Nice to see you too, buddy," Asher said, as he gave Eden's shoulder a shove.

"It would be nice to see you on time for once." Eden wasn't in the mood for Asher's banter tonight. A laugh escaped his friend, and Eden wanted to slug him one.

Mason cut in. "I think some beers are needed."

As he headed for the bar, the team chatted around Eden. He knew he was being a dick but couldn't be bothered with niceties. He hadn't been bothered for the last twelve months.

Flicking his gaze back to Luca and Evie, he pushed down the jealousy.

He'd been suspicious of her at the start. Putting her in the same group as Shylah, fast on his way to assuming all women were liars. She'd proven him wrong. Proven herself to be loyal. Her feelings for Luca were real, that much was obvious.

Mason returned with a round of beers. Eden took one, not caring that he'd downed the first too quickly. Other than finding everyone responsible for Project Arma, he didn't care about much these days.

"Any news on what happened to Troy's body?" The group quieted at Kye's question.

"We found nothing. His body was gone, the place cleaned up like he'd never been there. Like Luca and Evie were never there. No evidence on who raided Luca's house and stole Evie's laptop while they were at the hospital afterward, either. Betting my last dollar on it being his team, though." Frustration bled from Wyatt's voice.

"We know it was Carter and his boys. Everything happened too fast. They must've scrubbed the bunker, raided the house, then gone straight to Evie's hospital room." Bodie said what they all suspected.

Carter was the leader of the other SEAL team. Troy's team. The man who had attacked at the hospital while Evie was recovering.

Eden's jaw clenched at the memory of the assholes getting away. They'd been right there for the taking, and they'd slipped through his fingers. It damn near killed him to think about.

"We need to find them." He didn't hide his frustration.

"We're working on it," Mason promised. He'd been in that hospital room as well. No doubt he felt the same gut-clenching regret that they'd gotten away. They'd had a chance to make some people from Project Arma pay. Get information out of them, and they'd fucked it up.

"How could they have swiped the body, raided Luca's house, taken her laptop…all without leaving evidence?" Asher spoke the words quietly, but all seven men heard him.

"They were clean and efficient. It's nothing that we couldn't

219

do. The bigger question is, who's giving the orders?" Wyatt's hand tightened around his beer.

Oliver met Eden's gaze. "Commander Hylar."

The team was quiet for a moment. Hylar had been their commander, and they had trusted him with their lives. He'd been the one to volunteer them for Project Arma.

Being betrayed by him was like being betrayed by their father. It had hit them all hard.

They were guessing he'd received monetary incentives to hand over their team for the project. He also may have been providing weekly reports after training sessions on how effective the drugs were.

"We'll find him." Mason's voice was low and deadly.

"Then what?" The frustration inside Eden crested. Would they turn him in? Kill him? Would they want to?

Wyatt took a swig of his beer before he answered. "We'll deal with it then. One step at a time."

The team didn't speak for a moment. Eden's mind went back to the same place it always went. "What about Shylah? Find anything on her?" He hadn't asked about her location in a while. Every time he did, he held his breath, not sure if he wanted her found, or just hoped she'd stay hidden. Wyatt's response was always the same. There was never a trace.

This time, Wyatt hesitated.

Eden's heart sped up a fraction.

"There was a sighting of her. She was working at a hospital in Georgetown."

Eden's insides froze, even as a million emotions shot through him. "It was definitely her?"

"Yes. I confirmed the picture." Uncertainty filled Eden. He didn't know whether he felt relieved, anxious, or angry. He tried to calm himself as Wyatt continued. "She's not working there anymore, though. She handed in her resignation last week and left town."

The feeling of loss hit Eden hard. Shylah had been within reaching distance. Now she was gone again.

Motioning that he wanted out, he exited the booth after the others moved. "I'm going to head home."

He began walking, not waiting for a response. Shooting Luca a look, he saw his friend watching him. Eden didn't want to see the pity in his eyes. His brothers knew what Shylah had meant to him. How much her betrayal had cost him.

Pushing outside, he started walking toward his truck but was stopped by Wyatt's hand on his arm. Turning reluctantly, Eden waited for him to speak.

"Do you want me to find her, Eden? Now that we have a confirmed sighting, it won't be too hard to track her."

Did he want that? What would happen if Wyatt found her? He couldn't stomach handing her over to the authorities. He also wasn't going to get close to her and leave himself open to that kind of hurt again. So why *would* he want her found?

He had to let her go. He needed to focus on finding everyone else who'd had a part to play in Project Arma. That should be taking all his time and energy, not the woman who'd pretended to love him.

"No. I don't want you to find her."

Wyatt studied him for a moment before giving Eden a slight nod and walking back into the bar.

Eden's feet felt heavy as he finished walking the short distance to his truck. Getting in, he forced his mind off Shylah for the drive home.

He lived farther out than the other guys. He'd bought the house because he wanted quiet. Solitude. He didn't want to deal with neighbors every day. People were too much work. They asked too many questions about things that were none of their business.

Eden knew he'd made the right decision about Shylah. Why couldn't he get the damn woman out of his head, then? His hands tightened around the wheel as her face yet again popped into his head. Her laugh, her smile. She was always at the forefront of his mind. Like a damn cold that he couldn't get rid of.

They were *done*, dammit. There was no way to ever recover from what had happened.

Pulling his truck over to the side of the road, Eden slammed his fists against the wheel in frustration. How was he supposed to get over her when he didn't know the depth of her involvement? Why she'd chosen *him*? Why she'd said nothing, even at the very end? The last day he'd seen her, she'd woken up in his damn bed, as usual.

Pulling out his phone, he dialed Wyatt's number.

"Hunter?"

"Find her." Just two words. Then he hung up.

Sitting there a moment, he let that decision turn over in his mind, struggling to accept it. He *deserved* to know the truth. He needed answers. He needed to know why. Why did she pick him, make him love her, if she'd always planned to betray him?

Eden would find her—and the truth—even if it destroyed him.

Order Eden today!

ALSO BY NYSSA KATHRYN

PROJECT ARMA SERIES

Uncovering Project Arma

Luca

Eden

Asher

Mason

Wyatt

Bodie

Oliver

Kye

JOIN my newsletter and be the first to find out about sales and new releases!

https://www.nyssakathryn.com/vip-newsletter

ABOUT THE AUTHOR

Nyssa Kathryn is a romantic suspense author. She lives in South Australia with her daughter and hubby and takes every chance she can to be plotting and writing. Always an avid reader of romance novels, she considers alpha males and happily-ever-afters to be her jam.

Don't forget to follow Nyssa and never miss another release.

Facebook | Instagram | Amazon | Goodreads